DESPOT

GARVEY LOUISON

Dedicated to Einstein:

"He is a wise man who does not grieve for the things which he has not,

but rejoices for those which he has." – Epictetus

CONTENTS

CHAPTER ONE

The undulating mountainous countryside of Mabuya Island gives way to a dirt track snaking its way through the rural region. Two black Mitsubishi Pajero's and a 500 Mercedes-Benz Saloon pass through the lush green landscape of this secluded section of the island, imposing their unsolicited presence on the terrain.

The vehicles stop and several muscular men get out. They stand by as the diminutive Karl Stone climbs out. He walks around to the rear of the last SUV, where Swaggart is waiting with a vibrantly colored shirt in his hand. Karl removes his jacket, tie, and plain shirt and dons the colored shirt. Swaggart hitches the concealed weapon in his waistband before shadowing Karl back to his seat.

Karl squeezes past Swaggart's belly to climb into the front seat of the leading SUV.

"Watch that weight, Swaggart," Karl spits out.

"I am trying, boss," Swaggart mumbles.

Swaggart occupies the rear, and the other security officers scramble to redistribute themselves among the other vehicles.

They move along the rugged, dusty road to the town center of Caress.

As they enter the town, Karl observes people packed into open one-door shops, straining to get a peek at his convoy. Between the shops, people hang out of the windows of two-story houses to look at him. He lowers the dark-tinted window and waves to the onlookers. They return the compliment.

He watches a stray dog crossing the road. In its mouth is a chicken leg stolen from one of the food stalls that are everywhere—selling grilled fish, barbecued chicken, whelks and crabmeat, potato and breadfruit fries, and potent rum brews and bottles of lager chilled in giant coolers.

The sound systems belt out reggae and calypso music for the crowd who have come to hear Prime Minister Karl Stone, leader of the Mabuya National Party (MNP). Banners are swaying, and decorative buntings and flags flap in the breeze.

Young and old men and women make up the crowd. The children play hide-and-seek, running through the adults. Apart from the music blasting from the main sound system, several smaller systems scattered on the periphery play their own songs.

Karl inspects his shirt.

"Don't worry, boss," Swaggart says. "The shirt looks good."

"You sure?" Karl asks.

"Just right for the occasion." Swaggart places his fingers on his lips and blows a kiss in the wind.

"How me hair looking?" Karl asks.

Swaggart looks at Karl's low-cropped hair, the black dye disappearing at the roots to reveal an interceding grayish brown.

"Looking like a boss," Swaggart says. "Go out there and drop it on them like you accustomed to."

Word of Karl's arrival travels through the gathering, and the crowd becomes excited and noisy as the convoy penetrates. Karl waves as his SUV cruises through the crowd.

Jules Bourne, chairman of the meeting and the general secretary of the party, stands in front of the microphone on a small platform.

"Sisters and brothers, I have information that the Honorable Prime Minister Karl Stone is right here in this crowd."

"Karl! Karl! Karl! Karl! We want Karl! We want Karl! We want Karl!" the crowd shouts.

"We are happy, happy, happy working for the MNP!" Jules whips up a tempo. "Sing along with me!"

"We are happy, happy, happy working for the MNP!" the crowd chants.

The three vehicles are driven slowly through the crowd and come to a halt at the stage.

Swaggart clears the way for the security men to take up their respective lookout positions. Karl Stone emerges from the SUV, climbs the small stage, and makes his way to the podium.

"Sisters and brothers, I bring you the honorable prime minister, Karl Stone!" Jules Bourne announces.

Karl hugs and kisses Jules on both cheeks. Over the years, he has learned to trust Jules because Jules protects him, firmly believing that the party cannot move forward without Karl's leadership. Jules is focused and deliberate, a straight shooter who pulls no punches in the quest to get things done.

As Karl's right-hand man, he never makes his own decisions, and he ensures that others fulfill their end of the bargain when it comes to matters of the MNP. Party members know Jules has Karl's blessing whenever tasks are distributed.

"Yeah, yeah, yeah! Karl, Karl, Karl!" the crowd roars.

Karl stands at the podium waving to his minions and making no effort to stop the ruckus. He soaks in the energy before speaking.

"Welcome! Welcome, one and all from the Caress town center and surrounding areas." Karl surveys the gathering. "My friends, lovely to see you here this afternoon. I welcome you with my heart. Welcome to the fold of the MNP." He spreads his arms as if to embrace his audience.

"We are happy, happy working for the MNP! Oh, how happy we shall be, working for the MNP!" He leads the crowd in a chant, then raises his hand for them to settle down.

"Sisters and brothers, I will be brief. When I leave here, I have two other meetings to attend before going home. My friends, let me remind you that we have come a long way. Today we can boast that our democracy is at an advanced stage. Today you can walk the streets of Mabuya without fear. You can travel overseas whenever you want. Being a Mabuyan is something to be proud of. Our people hold their heads up high in the world.

"My friends, today you can get a job based on your qualifications and not sexual favors. Your sons and daughters can go to university because we have scholarships available, and you do not have to support my party to get them.

"My friends, we have started a new era. Gone are the days when you lived under a dictatorship. Dictatorship is dead."

"Dictatorship is dead...! Dictatorship is dead...! Dictatorship is dead!" the people echo. "We want Karl! We want Karl! KARL!"

"My friends, today we have democratic institutions to take care of your needs. We have investors pouring into our country with money to spend. There will be jobs for everyone. You shall hunger no more.

"Sisters and brothers, as I leave you this evening, remember that my door is always open. Come to me anytime; I will address your problems. I promise to do my best to find a solution. Allow no one to stop you from coming.

"Good evening, my dear people, and enjoy the rest of your activities."

Karl waves at the crowd as their screams rise into the air.

He steps from the stage and walks to the SUV brought forward to meet him.

"Come and take a drink!" someone shouts.

Karl obliges and he and Swaggart walk past the vehicle, making their way to the bar at the edge of the gathering. Side by side, they merge with the patrons followed by two members of the security detail. The other officers stay with the vehicles.

Perched on the edge of the town's seafront, Yellow's Bar is a two-story town house over two hundred years old. Once the home of the town council during the colonial era, it was sold by the government as the importance of the council faded.

Large beams support the upper floor over the open-plan bar and domino tables. Past the bar are the kitchen and storeroom with a back door leading into an open yard and the rugged sea. Yellow cooks and brews homemade beer and wines there. He insists on using 100 percent local products in his concoctions.

His theory is simple. You may chat on a dry throat but never drink on an empty stomach. In minutes, he can whip up chicken and sweet potato chips, fish and cassava bakes, or shark and homemade coo-coo. Other days, he cooks a full meal.

Yellow lives upstairs. Thick, heavy curtains show through the slot windows with built-in hurricane covers.

There is parking for six vehicles outside.

The men in the shop step aside as Karl approaches.

Karl pauses for a moment at seeing Ras sitting on a stool in the corner. He had not seen the little Rasta man in fifty years.

"How long you been hiding in the bush up here?" Karl asks.

"Up here me father from," Ras replies.

"You traveled from here every day to come to school in the city?" Karl is curious.

"No. I boarded in town during the week and came back here on weekends."

"You must check me. I could give you a job," Karl says.

"Thank you but no thanks. I man happy how ah is. I live off farming and craft making." Ras strokes his beard.

Karl looks away from Ras and turns to Yellow. He recoils as the images on the wall behind the barman pop out at him—portraits of Fidel Castro, Che Guevara, Maurice Bishop, and Bob Marley. None of him.

"Good to see you, boss," Yellow says from behind the counter.

"Nice to be here again," Karl replies. He knows Yellow to be his supporter, but he also knows the man to be independent, opinionated, well-read, and intelligent. Yellow's loyalties can shift fluidly. This is no blind supporter.

He met Yellow fifteen years before. The six-foot-seven-inch albino appeared from nowhere and bought the old town house with cash. The story was that he retired as an executive in Microsoft Corporation and chose Mabuya Island as his final resting place.

At seventy going on thirty-five, Yellow is not the typical barman. He is soft-spoken and clearly expresses his mind without fear. He is versed in history, chemistry, engineering, town and country planning, agriculture, agro-processing, and current affairs. He lectures his customers on cleanliness, self-respect, empathy, emotional intelligence, leadership, wealth creation, mixing drinks, cooking, food presentation, the art of war, kung fu, guns, games, sports, and the importance of maintaining respect for the laws of the land. He is a walking library.

He told Karl that his role is to entertain, impart knowledge, and be an example to others in the community. Throughout his life, people taught him to be ethical, professional, and independent. These are the qualities he wishes to impart to the citizens who come to his bar.

Yellow wanted to lift the art of bartending to a higher standard. He resented the notion that a barman took the job only because he had nowhere else to go. People on Mabuya viewed bartending as a job for the uneducated and academic failures in society. He wanted to change that perception.

The bartender must be an all-rounder. Throw him into the ring daily with lawyers, doctors, accountants, politicians, teachers, and would-be intellectuals, and he can hold his own. Despite the old talk, he must remember to serve the patrons. Keep the drinks and food flowing with love and affection.

Yellow reaches into his cooler and pulls out a beer in a green bottle and offers it to Karl.

"Just the right thing, my brother," Karl says. "Glad things are working out well."

Yellow had convinced Karl of the importance of the bartender to society. Their work wasn't just about mixing drinks. They must know the chemistry of mixing, and therefore, the government needed to train and certify them. The operating rules must be standard, as local and foreign patrons will consume their creations.

For Karl, bartenders were frontline interface to tourists. The impressions they give could have a lasting impact on tourism. He agreed with training and standardizing operations. That way, he could boast about consumers demanding more and holding bartenders to a greater standard of building communities and maintaining health and sanitation.

"Yes, man," Yellow agrees. "You're working things out, and you're always in this town. One thing they cannot fault you for is dat. You're not like the opposition boys."

Karl puts the green bottle to his lips, and Yellow smiles.

"I know that's your favorite. Why don't you allow it to come into the country legally?" "Listen, man," Karl whispers. "As long as they pay duties, I turn a blind eye. Let us be realistic; I need money to run the country. If I get, you get. If I don't have, you will starve. They can call it contraband or any other name. As long as they pay their dues, we're good."

"Good." Yellow laughs. "You're the man."

"How are things, really?" Karl asks.

"Great," Yellow claims. "They can't touch you."

"You hypocrite bitch, tell the man the truth!" Ras shouts from his corner.

"Ras, chill." Yellow swats his hand. "Big people having a drink."

"Things not okay," Ras bellows. "I doh ha wuk."

"Ras, last week there was roadwork."

"You call that wuk?" Ras shouts. "You call cutting bush by the road, wuk? I call it modern-day slavery. Shackles on the mind."

"My friend, things are happening." Karl turns to Ras. "We have money coming in."

"Me nah you fren!" Ras shouts. "An me nah want u money. You a liar and a false prophet. You ah bring dis country to the gutter, to the dawgs."

"It is your opinion, my brother," Karl says.

"Me nah u brother!" Ras shouts again. "Screw you, Karl. You messing up."

"Aye. Aye, watch you language, Ras," Yellow intervenes. "Do not disrespect the prime minister."

Karl downs the beer in two gulps and slams the bottle on the counter.

"I will see you." He taps Yellow on his back and turns to leave the shop, greeting a few people as he hustles to the waiting vehicles.

Karl climbs into the rear seat of the trailing SUV, leans back, and exhales.

"You guys didn't sweep that blasted shop?" he snaps.

"We saw him there," one of the security men says.

"And you let me go in there?" Karl snaps again.

"I know him; he does not usually act that way," another guard claims.

"Everybody expects me to make work for them. Let them get off their ass and help themselves. Lazy," Karl snarls. "I am going home. I have had enough for today."

"So early, boss?" the driver asks.

"Yeah, home."

The convoy leaves the crowd for the open road. Karl rolls down the window to inhale fresh air and gaze at the Mabuyan countryside: the hills rolling into the beaches merging with the setting sun on the horizon.

***

After Karl leaves, Yellow leans over the counter and looks at Ras.

"You must be so embarrassing?" he asks.

"I have my views," Ras answers. "He has his. Yellow, let me tell you about this man. Since we were in form one, he say he go be the prime minister of this country. We asked him, what made him believe that? He said his mother told him so. His mother knew what to do to make him the prime minister."

"His mother?" Yellow asks. "I thought he was close to his father?"

"This man hates his father. He feels his father cheated on his mother. The father has a pile ah children outside he marriage. His mother had to vend in the market to take care of him and his younger brother. One day we playing in the schoolyard, and Karl smash the game. We chase him through the town until he gets to the vendors' market. This is how I know he mother is a witch. Karl run straight to her; she lift up her dress, and Karl disappears. At the same time, we freeze in we tracks. None of us could move. Then the woman put down she dress. All of us had to turn around and flee to the schoolyard."

"Ras, you make up that story."

"Everyone who was there that day remembers that incident. Six of us chase the man through the town."

"You don't like him, and you hate his mother."

"Yellow, me nah deal with no iniquity woman. Woman who worship Satan for she son to progress in society."

"I agree, but you could have allowed him to come and go from here like another citizen."

"You damn right. That's what he will be after the elections."

"That is not what the latest poll says."

"I don't believe in polls. They are biased."

Yellow reaches under the counter and pulls out a newspaper.

"This paper have him winning 55 percent of the votes with eight out of ten seats."

"He own the people who printing that."

"You know that's not true. He and Errol been fighting each other for years."

"What the paper say about the situation in the country?"

Yellow flips through the newspaper, selects an article, and reads.

"Karl and his MNP have succeeded in splitting the country down the middle. In the last election the ruling party won all ten seats in the House of Representatives with a meager 51 percent of the votes cast in the election. Although amassing 49 percent of the votes, the opposition failed to translate that into seats.

Further analysis revealed that more than 30 percent of eligible voters stayed home and refused to exercise their franchise and vote in the general election. This meant that the MNP continued in power for the next five years as they had done for the last fifteen.

The ruling party has thrived on the youthful population whose main objective has been instant gratification. They bear no allegiance to the past. The ruling party in its last election campaign used the latest reggae and soca stars to woo the population to attend massive rallies and zonal meetings, chanting for the party. The party poured financial resources into fanciful displays of exuberance at every opportunity. They outshone and outspent the opposition at every turn.

The current poll is showing if elections were called today the MNP would return to power, winning all eleven seats in the House of Representatives."

CHAPTER TWO

On the other side of the island, Victor Calliste, the seventy-year-old leader of the opposition party, the Mabuya Democratic Movement (MDM), is waiting to address a crowd at the Full Moon Playing Field.

The general secretary of the party, Aadesh Hamid, is addressing the crowd. At fifty, Aadesh, a civil engineer, is considered the natural replacement for Victor.

"Sisters and brothers, I know you didn't come here to listen to me," Aadesh says. "The man you have come to listen to is sitting right here. Behind me.

"Let me tell you about this man. He will sacrifice his soul for this country. Many years ago, at the helm of his professional career as an attorney at law, this man was challenged by the establishment. They challenged him to make a choice. Give up your struggle on behalf of the people of Mabuya, or go to prison. Sisters and brothers, for most people, this would be a no-brainer. For example, one of my friends says, 'Darling, I love you. I will die for you, but I will not go to jail for you.'

"For our political leader and the next prime minister of this country, the choice was straightforward. He chose going to prison. They kept him locked up for four years. You know how he survived? He has a strong mind and a good heart.

"Sisters and brothers, sing with me: *For he's a jolly good fellow, for he's a jolly good fellow, and this I can't deny. Sing it again. For he's a jolly good fellow, for he's a jolly good fellow, and this I can't deny.*

"Sisters and brothers, I bring to you our party leader, mentor, defender, and future prime minster, Victor Calliste!"

Victor strides purposefully toward the podium. He passes his fingers over his shock of gray hair and studies his audience before addressing them.

"Thank you, Brother Aadesh. I know that with you around, the future of our party is in good hands.

"Members on the platform, sisters and brothers. Welcome. I heard some people, even members of the executive of our party, saying we win already. This is incorrect. We have a fight on our hands. We must be prepared. Not only must we win, but we need a resounding victory to get rid of this man called Karl Stone once and for all. Let us stand and defend our country."

He looks over the sea of faces to the waves bashing against the defense wall. He wonders what effect the sea would have had on the coastline without the construction of the wall. His gaze takes him from the ocean to the mountain that tapers off into the valley floor.

He knows that sea-level rise is a result of climate change. The estimates, which show the sea level rising by three feet within the next century with a possibility of six to ten feet in extreme cases, mean that small island countries, like Mabuya Island, will be devastated by a rise of even two feet.

A chill runs through his body as he thinks about this and the shrinking supply of fresh water from the lessening of groundwater sources and rainfall. This compromised water supply will place pressure on any already fragile agricultural industry. Mabuya was already experiencing a reduction in soil fertility and soil degradation.

Small island states like Mabuya will suffer from changes in the water cycle, groundwater contamination, higher sea levels, and seawater pollution. In turn, this will change social and economic operations within the islands as people's standard of living is degraded.

He finds the subject complex and unpredictable. All small island states will not be affected the same way. The water levels will rise at different rates. The impact on Mabuya will depend on its natural defenses, mangrove forests, coral reefs, and coastal defenses. There will be erosion, flooding, and water settlement in new areas of the coastline.

In Mabuya, most of the housing, agricultural land, the airport, bridges, ports, and roads are on the coastline. They are certainly in for a ride.

He hitches his trousers, flicks his suspenders, and tightens his grip on the podium. Through the rims of his silver-lined glasses, he locks eyes with an old woman in the front row.

"My friends, let me explain what I consider the worst-case scenario. Karl Stone has no conscience, no sense of right and wrong. There is no repentance in his heart. He goes to church every Sunday, but he knows no God. We do not want him back."

Again, Victor checks out the crowd. This time a young man a few rows back becomes his target.

"Do you want him?" Victor asks.

"No!" the crowd shouts.

"Do you want him?" he repeats.

"No!" the crowd choruses.

"You know me. I have been in business for the past forty years in this town, and no one can say I have mistreated them. No one can say they came for help and I did not help or point them in the right direction. I will never accept dirty money to further my cause. These crooks and con artists can take their money and stick it you know where.

"Someone questioned Karl Stone about a crook investor. Do you know what he said?"

Victor pauses; all eyes in the crowd are focused on him, like thirsty donkeys being drawn to the river.

"The man said, 'Bring more. Keep them coming.' These are the men he likes. My friends, can you imagine the audacity of Karl Stone? This man is unfit to continue to lead this country. Come Election Day, November fourth, we will vote him out. We will send him back to where he belongs. Crying in the arms of his wicked mother. If he thinks her obeah would save him this time, he'd better think again. Tell him I say our righteousness and faith in the Almighty is stronger than his obeah.

"He relies on crooked business arrangements to finance his election campaign and remain in office. His most recent business arrangement involves a fugitive from Ukraine, a former double-agent spy called Milosevic. The world wants Milosevic. They want him for espionage, bribery, forgery, and money laundering, just to name a few. He spent four years in prison in Panama."

The chairman of the meeting hands Victor a folder. He thanks the chairman and holds the folder up for the crowd to see.

"My people, if you don't believe me, check out this file with a summary of the criminal activities of Milosevic. I can give you copies.

"My friends, as a nation we need to make up our minds. Here and now, I challenge you to decide who you are supporting. Will you be on the side of corruption and con artists, or are you law-abiding citizens willing to develop this country with honesty, integrity, and hard work?

"We reject Karl Stone and his philosophy. We reject his way of life. Vote him out. Join me. Join the movement against Karl Stone. Just like a manicou on top of a coconut tree, we will juke him down. We will juke him, we will juke him down."

The crowd laughs and joins.

"We will juke him, we will juke him down!

"We will juke him, we will juke him down!

"Just like a manicou on top a coconut tree, we will juke him down!"

Victor returns to his seat to resounding applause.

***

Back in the town center, Jules closes the meeting and looks on as the crowd scatters. He times his move and slides away through the back of the stage, limbering to his parked vehicle. The driver sits in the SUV with the engine running and the air conditioner cooling the interior.

"Let's go," Jules commands as he enters.

The driver engages the drivetrain of the Land Rover LR2, teasing the accelerator and steering gingerly for the machine to pick its way through the dissipating crowd. They leave the crowded car park and enter the main street in the town. People bang on the darkened window to attract Jules's attention, but he ignores them.

Jules realizes that the party has started. Supporters of the MNP are milling around buying drinks and food, talking loudly and gyrating to the pumped-up music from the deejay. He knows that entering this melee will cost him time and money.

As a politician of thirty years, Jules is aware of his distinct personalities. His public figure is the one who chairs meetings of the political party, campaigns during the general election, and walks from house to house to ask for votes on Election Day. The other personality is the shy architectural engineer who prefers to lock himself away working on plans, drawings, and projects.

At the edge of the main street, Jules leans back in the Recaro seat as the driver increases acceleration and heads out of the town. They take the longer dry road along the coastline to avoid the mountainous rain forest.

They speed by the small wooden houses paced out along the seaside—a community that depends on craft making, fishing, and farming for its livelihood. He smiles as he realizes that the natural resources for Mabuya's magical existence are at hand: the wild pine trees for craft making; agricultural land and freshwater for farming; the sea for oceanic explorations and coastal fisheries; and mangroves, which give matting material and food.

He leans forward and adjusts the air conditioner. It's freezing, but he doesn't want to lower the windows. The automatic transmission shifts seamlessly as the vehicle settles into the terrain. The hardy wild pine trees with their long leaves, ideal for weaving, form a natural fence line between the houses. Jules knows that low income and limited access to government financial support explain the high levels of household food inadequacy. Most people lack access to personal transportation and sanitation conveniences within the community.

Jules's uncle was a craft maker. This man could weave any product from a bale of cured grass. He used a variety of grass, plant leaves, and vines to produce his art. Jules remembers walking to the forest with him to collect the suitable raw materials. They would make several trips and store their finds under the house for curing.

His uncle conditioned the straw by cutting and placing it into a container of water to soak and then running the strands through a piece of old cloth to remove excess moisture before weaving straws.

Jules would sit on a bench as his uncle fastened the ends to form a base, then worked his way upward, alternating between clockwise and counterclockwise turns until the required shape emerged. Other times he used a mold, working his way around the shape to achieve the desired pattern.

His uncle would tuck the final straws into shape and sit back to admire his work before commencing another masterpiece. He created goblet holders, baskets, bags, hats, picture frames, brooms, door mats, and a range of other products in his makeshift workshop under the house. They sold in the village and sometimes traveled to the city to deliver pre-orders. No one in the family took up the skill after the death of his uncle. Jules wonders if life might give him time to test his skills.

The LR2 responds smoothly to the bumpy road. Jules had purchased the HSE LUX version. He prefers European vehicles for their build and spaciousness. The self-leveling, multi-link suspension softens the holes and ragged edges of the road surface as the driver cuts speed. They turn into a yard, the permanent all-wheel drive grappling with the gravel and loose dirt in the driveway before the driver stops.

Jules steps out and walks toward the house ahead. Over the years, he had expanded and strengthened the house from its original design. He imagines how challenging it was to build a house on this estate during his father's time. Money and transportation were hard to come by. His father had done the original design and most of the construction. He died when Jules was eight, leaving a wife and three other children. Jules was the last.

The house sits on twelve acres of farmland and is a one-hour drive from the city center.

Jules looks at the overgrown grass and unkempt fence and makes a mental note to send the maintenance people.

The housekeeper opens the door.

"Good evening," Jules says.

"Hi, Jules," she says, stepping aside to allow him to pass. "She is expecting you."

"How are you keeping?" Jules asks.

"I am doing fine," she says, smiling.

"Always doing fine," he mumbles.

He walks past the housekeeper and enters the living room, a long through lounge with a daybed near the window, a locally made two-piece sitting room set, and farther along, a hardwood six-seater dining table. Five doors lead to each bedroom, including the master bedroom. They made most of the house from local natural materials, just as his father loved.

The kitchen is a refectory with counters made from local stones. Jules had maintained the old fireplaces after each renovation even though his mother didn't cook on wood fires anymore. He laid out the tables and barstools randomly. One sits in an indoor courtyard while the host dishes out breakfast in a zigzag pattern.

Jules had replaced the earth floor with concrete and ceramic tiles. He had maintained the slots at the top of each wall originally meant to allow woodsmoke and hot air out under the high concrete ceiling. A row of coconut and banana trees shade the kitchen. During breakfast, the sunshine casts arcs onto the floor and solid surfaces, creating a soft divine light.

During his father's years, foreign materials were scarce. Jules vowed to keep the local part of his renovation as a tribute to his father's legacy. His architectural training made him conscious of his interest in using a blend of materials—local and imported. When in doubt, he erred on the side of locally available items. He loves hardwood, oven-baked bricks, stone, and reclaimed materials from old houses.

"You are welcome, son," his mother greets him.

"I thought it might be late," he answers and walks to the figure sitting on the daybed. She has lost more weight since the last time he saw her. From a normal 108 pounds, she is now under one hundred. He sees the loose skin on her face and around her neck.

"I came from a meeting; I rushed to get here," he explains.

"I want to change my supplies," she tells him.

"Let me help you."

"That will be great. Help me get inside."

Jules takes her by the hand and leads her toward the master bedroom. He maintains her stock level by checking with the housekeeper periodically to make sure she never runs out of supplies.

At each step, she drags the wheeled stand carrying the supply bag for her dialysis. The early signs of her failing kidneys quickly worsened with time. After consultations with the kidney specialist and her family doctor, they had agreed to do peritoneal dialysis at home. Jules flinched when the doctors explained this method of dialysis, which uses the lining of the belly to filter waste and extra fluid from the body. He had silently twirled the word in his mouth—the *peritoneum*, the lining surrounding the abdominal cavity and replacing part of the kidney function.

They get to the room, and his mother sits on the edge of the bed. Jules lifts her blouse and examines the catheter. She'd undergone minor surgery to insert the catheter into the abdomen.

"The catheter looks fine," he tells her.

"Then it's only to change the bag," she says tiredly.

Jules leaves his mother for a moment and walks to the bedroom now used as a storage room for his mom's boxes of dialysis solution. He selects a bag of new fluid from an open box. For him, the choice of this method of dialysis was easy. This way, his mother has control over her treatments, doesn't need help to do her exchanges, didn't need a machine, plus she can move around and change at her convenience. They trained her for this a few times, and she picked it up quickly.

He bounces back to his mother and removes the drain bag and shuts off that line. He hooks the new bag onto the stand and connects it to the catheter. They watch as the dialysis solution flows from a bag into a tube through the catheter and into the abdominal cavity.

"All done," he says. He goes to the toilet and empties the drain bag, discarding the bag in a waste bucket; cleans up; and returns to his mom.

"Great. The housekeeper will wipe me before I go to sleep. I will do my readings and prayers, then she will tuck me in until God is ready for me," she says.

"You have a long time still, Mom. You are as strong as a monkey's tail." He laughs softly.

"You always had faith and courage, son," she says.

"I know you will make it," he reassures her.

"Thanks for stopping by. I didn't get to thank you for the supply boxes you sent this week," she says.

"That is the least I can do. I will come by again soon. If you need anything, call me." He bends over and kisses her on the cheeks. He walks to the door and says goodbye to the housekeeper.

"Home," he orders as he enters the vehicle.

The driver eases the vehicle out of the yard. Jules reflects on his visit with his mother as the least he can do at this point. Among the many occasions that she supported him in the past, he recalls the period when he was setting off to study. He had paid the university fees but needed spending money and a final payment to secure his plane ticket. An argument erupted in the family over his choice of London as a place to study and architecture as his interest.

His mother disappeared into her room and returned with a small plastic bag that she squeezed into his hand. He was on his way.

Architecture came naturally to him, like a gift from his father. Jules wanted to design structures that conserved material and land use while supporting sound design and modernity. At university in London, he discovered that in many countries, architecture is considered art. By extension, art is considered subversive. The army and police destroy books and literature that go against their ideals. London instructed him in the mix of modernity and the ancient. The computer generated and the sculpted. A visual outlet for the traditional and the classical. During vacation he used to take the ferry from Dover, England, to Calais, France, and back-packed his way through the European Union on a budget.

He designs with energy and enthusiasm, from small low-cost buildings on a mingy budget to massive over-the-top structures requiring money and innovation. He uses computer imaging but always performs the finishing manually.

During his travels in Europe, Jules formed the view that there was a relationship between construction and dictatorship. Germany's autobahn was his best example. To him, this modern marvel of roadway was inconceivable without the dictatorship of Adolph Hitler. To him construction is expensive, and only a dictator would marshal funds for a monument for admiration long after he dies. In local parlance, "He who has the most oil will fry the most bake"—a saying his father repeated throughout his life.

Jules smiles, recalling graduating from the engineering-focused architecture program and the immense potential he saw in returning to Mabuya. His first job was to manage a government-owned mining and quarrying company. Karl recruited him to join his party, then in opposition. The MNP won the next election, and Jules was sworn in as minister of infrastructure. His first task was to attack the broken infrastructure in the country. He had always detested the unpaved roads with animals wandering across, causing accidents. Karl's priority was to build a sports stadium and the prime ministerial complex with funding from South Korea.

Jules acknowledges the strange dynamic between Karl and him. Karl sees him as his student and treats him with rare respect, nurturing and training him. During their disagreements Karl asks him to pause and think matters over, even though Karl's view will ultimately prevail. With other ministers, Karl dismisses their suggestions outright.

Jules's smile broadens. While on the outside people see them as inseparable—an evil fraternal twin constantly plotting ways to inflict suffering upon the masses, he knows they are unaware of the internal battles between Karl and him. They don't know the frustrations Jules endures.

The LR2 pulls up to the electric gate, and the driver presses the remote control. He waits until the gate opens fully, then drives slowly toward the house.

***

Karl's convoy enters a cul-de-sac and slows down when passing through a housing area. He is on his way to visit his mother, Rita Stone. They drive past a mixture of single-room ply houses and bigger middle-income detached homes. The upscale houses contain verandahs, parking facilities, extra floors, and adjoining land.

They pass the recreation center, church, small shops, and a motor vehicle garage. Karl returns a wave from a workman at the garage. Steel pan players practice their music at a nearby pan house.

They pull into Rita's yard. Her house is a single-story bungalow with the parking level lower than the verandah. A low roof covers the verandah and main entrance, while six concrete columns support the main roof, forming an observation deck surrounded by decorated precast concrete balusters.

The kitchen is visible through two unobstructed windows on either side of the double entrance doors. More windows and jalousies occupy the entire sides and ends of the hall. Heavy drapes shield the living and dining room. When the drapes are opened, blinds made of angled slats diffuse the light and allow a breeze to sweep through the home.

The security men exit the vehicles and form a cordon to cover Karl. He passes through and climbs the short steps into the verandah of the house.

Rita's long flowery dress blows in the breeze. At five feet tall, she weighs less than a hundred pounds. She beams as Karl walks into her open arms. She ushers him inside, and they head to the six-seater dining table he bought for her more than forty years ago. He wanted to eat in comfort whenever he visited her, whether alone or with friends.

Karl's younger brother, Kenny, is seated and eating.

"We cooked your favorite today," Rita says. "Green pea soup."

"Just what I need." He pulls up a chair and sits.

Karl is amazed that at ninety-two his mother moves as if she is less than half her age. All her life, she has never been to a doctor. Her wiry, preserved body is a wound-up spring. Her gray hair, though thinning at the top, is thick and strong beneath her head-tie, which matches her dress. He draws inspiration and energy from her.

When at her house, he and Kenny know who is in charge. She is domestic, calm, and sociable. But she is also the boss, directly involved in Karl's life, leading the way in his protection and defense.

Karl is now seventy-two years old. He wonders if he might live to be her age or die early like his father, in his seventies. If he leaves politics, he can enjoy the rest of his life—simple and normal, like Rita's.

The maid places the bowl of hot green pea soup in front of Karl. He lifts a spoonful. Too hot, he decides.

"How was your day, Karl?" Rita asks, her fiery brown eyes drilling into him.

"Great."

"That's not what I want to hear. What's troubling my son?"

"Elections."

"But they are not due yet."

"They might force me to call it early."

"Why?"

"I must change certain people on my team. Those who are not performing. You know who they are. Two of them are against me. They do not support my philosophy and my views on moving this country forward. Mom, I refuse to harbor people around me who are against me. Another two are lazy and do not want to work. I spoke to them several times about the importance of going out there and putting in the political work. Working with the party groups at the village level. They only want to posture and enjoy the benefits of being government ministers."

Karl has some soup.

"I will pray they leave you alone."

"I am thinking of leaving politics."

"That, you cannot do."

"Why, Mom?"

"Who will lead this country?"

"There must be other people."

"No, son, there is no one else." She moves closer to him and rests her hand on his shoulders. "You were born to lead."

"But I am getting old. I need to consider my life."

"This is your life. You are not getting old. Look at me. Every day I get stronger."

She does a little dance while walking to the sink.

"Remember, my father died at seventy-four."

"He was a weakling. He wore out his body. Too many women," says Rita.

"Mommy?" Karl chokes on his soup.

"He had the only mill in the village where the women came to grind corn. He would have sex with them and not charge them the right price. I saw him with my own eyes. Look at him today."

Karl erupts in laughter.

"Mom, are you joking?"

"I swear to God. I cannot lie on a dead man."

They all burst out laughing.

"Your mother is right. You cannot let us go now," the maid joins in.

"I know I am right."

"Follow your heart," Kenny says. "I will support you."

Karl trusts Kenny, who wants only Karl's good, nothing for himself. He is a slim, short man with cropped, dyed-black hair. His lean chest is visible through his half-buttoned cotton shirt.

Kenny is a perfectionist, a man of ethics. He is self-righteous and loves to be right. He focuses on solving big problems because he pays attention to details. For him, life must be stable and under control.

Karl feels Kenny needs to be nonjudgmental; unlike Karl, he abides by the rules—for the most part. Karl is reluctant to talk to him about certain things—he can't tell him everything. Kenny might freeze up and become uncomfortable.

Karl finishes his meal in silence. He kisses Rita goodbye before joining his security men outside.

CHAPTER THREE

Allyson Calliste is in her cherished kitchen preparing dinner. Her favorite design aspect of the long farmhouse-style kitchen is the lounge effect with the island and bar transforming into the dining section. The utensils hanging at random over the workstation create a sense of rustic disorder.

She is wearing loose shorts and a cotton vest while peeling fruits to make a smoothie. She pops a piece of mango into her mouth and looks at her children, Clint and Cari, sitting at the bar. A car pulls into the yard.

"That must be your father."

She follows the shuffle of feet as the children disappear from the kitchen. They hide in the broom closet along the hallway.

Victor had a fit when she installed a five-burner cooker, a French door refrigerator, chrome faucets, and a pair of mesmeric mirrors. Although they were on sale, he had complained that she'd busted the budget with her expensive taste. Later, he appreciated it. Four windows flooded light into the workspace. The layout of the appliances and cabinets were practical and reachable.

White countertops trimmed with black edges balanced the light. A local joiner built the floating shelves, the bar, and the island, and she saved money off the retail prices by going with appliances from a scratch-and-dent sale.

With her mind on preparing the fruits, she is surprised when Victor sneaks up and embraces her from behind.

"Where are the children?" he asks.

"I dunno." She wriggles her bottom against him.

"We have the house to ourselves."

"Um-hmm." Her mouth is filled with fruits.

He draws her in tighter. "Bye, smoothie."

"Um-hmm." She swallows and turns to kiss him.

"Daddy, Daddy."

They pull apart as the children jump out of the cupboard and race into the kitchen.

"Hi, you two."

Allyson smiles at him.

"Let me change my clothes," he tells them. "I will be back for dinner."

"See you, Daddy," Cari says as she jostles with Clint for a chair at the dining table. At six, she is strong and determined. Clint's two advanced years are not obvious. They are in the same class at school with Cari threatening to move ahead of her elder brother.

Allyson blends the smoothie, pours out two tumblers, and finishes setting up the table. She lays out roasted chicken with fried potato chips for the children and grilled fish with garlic toasted bread for Victor and herself. She sets the kettle to boil for their afternoon tea.

Victor returns to join three sets of hungry eyes.

"How was it?" Allyson asks.

"I think we are gaining momentum," he says.

"People can be deceitful."

"I know, but I saw something in their eyes. They are hungry for change."

"What do you mean?"

"It's a resolution. A determination."

"To do what?"

"To kick this guy out of office. Hopefully, they are ready to change the current administration."

"You need to find out."

"We are doing the background research. The polls are showing us slightly behind at this point."

"Daddy, we have a field trip tomorrow," Cari announces.

"Where will you guys be going?"

"We go past the prison, the fort, and back to school."

"That will be very informative," Victor says.

"When we get back, we have to write about our trip," Clint says.

"You will show us what you write."

"Yes," they sing in unison.

"But, Daddy, do I have to go?" Cari asks.

"Of course. It is part of your schoolwork," Victor says.

"I don't want to go." Cari frowns.

"Why not?" Victor is curious.

"I don't like the prison."

"Why not?"

"Isn't the prison a place for evil men?" she asks.

"The trip is compulsory. You are going," Victor snaps.

They end their meal quietly.

"You guys know the drill. Take a bath, brush your teeth, and get ready for bed. I will come to tuck you in."

"Yes, Daddy," they answer, jumping off their chairs and running away.

Allyson clears the table and pauses.

"Why don't you tell them?" she asks.

"They are too young," he tells her, tears welling up in his eyes. "When they get older."

"I hope no one tells them before you do." She shakes her head.

***

Karl sits at the edge of the bed; he is stripped to his boxers and a white T-shirt. He yawns and sighs from the effects of a long day. Michelle is reading the Bible. She is in her silk nightgown, propped up against the raised top half of the bed, cushioned by fluffy pillows.

"You're really going again tonight?" Michelle asks from behind the Bible.

"Ah tell you to mind your own blasted business, woman," Karl snaps.

"Is she worth it?" Michelle presses on in a monotone as if Karl has not answered.

"You stay out of that," Karl growls.

She lowers the Bible.

"Risking your marriage? Your government?"

"Don't bring my government into this."

"I could expose you."

"You wouldn't do that."

"Keep on testing my faith."

"You have too much to lose."

"What if I don't care anymore?"

"You?" Karl heads to the bathroom, slamming the door behind him.

In front of the mirror, he removes his teeth, applies a solution, then washes them under the tap.

"This frigging woman," he mutters to himself in the mirror.

He leaves his teeth on the bathroom ledge, strips himself naked, and climbs into the shower.

***

Victor is kneeling on the floor next to the bed reading a bedtime story to Cari. He flicks the page and looks at his daughter. She matches his stare. He lowers the book, deciding to tell her a version of the story: "This is a story about the vivid imagination of Peter. In life you must have imagination. It isn't lying. It's your ability to dream and build a full story around that dream."

"Peter tells Wendy, the only girl of the three Darling children and his favorite, that he and Tinker Bell live in Neverland with the lost boys, boys who had fallen out of their baby carriages and were never found again.

He, begs Wendy and her brothers to go back to Neverland with him, promises to teach them to fly. After a little practice, they all fly out the window, barely escaping their parents and Nana, who has broken her chain to warn Mr. and Mrs. Darling of the danger to the children.

In Neverland, the Indians, with their chief and their princess, help to protect the lost boys against a group of mean pirates led by Captain Hook, who has a hook where one of his hands used to be. Hook wants to capture

Pan, for Peter is the one who tore off Hook's arm and fed it to a crocodile. The crocodile so liked the taste of the arm that he now follows Hook everywhere, waiting for a chance to eat the rest of him.

The crocodile has, unhappily, also swallowed a clock, and its ticking warns Hook whenever the crocodile approaches."

Victor looks at Cari again, and she is fast asleep. Before he leaves, he kisses her on the forehead and switches off the lights.

In the master bedroom, Allyson, her back propped against the headboard, is fiddling with her phone.

"Is she asleep?"

"Out for the count," he says. "Did you check on Clint?"

"Sound asleep a long time ago."

"How was your day, darling?"

"The children in school are campaigning for elections."

"Elections?"

"Every election cycle, they have their own version in school. Their own mock vote. They choose their party leader and candidates to mount a campaign."

"How long do they campaign?"

"They campaign for two weeks, then they vote."

"Is the voting along party lines or for individuals?"

"The campaign by party and vote by party."

"Do you think the results are a reflection of the society?"

"They have predicted every election result since we started fifteen years ago."

"When is the vote?"

"In two days by secret ballot."

"Instructive."

"When will you tell the children about your time in prison?"

"Soon."

"If you don't, I will."

"Leave it alone." He leans over and kisses her on the lips. "See you in the morning."

He lies in the dark, his eyes wide open. He remembers his arrest one Saturday morning. He had come from a meeting with two others in which they had discussed the launch of an anti-government newspaper. The week before, they had teased the ground with a version of the paper. The government sent them a warning to cease and desist. At the meeting that morning, they voted two to one to continue publishing.

He was descending the steps of the building when three military vehicles pulled up and soldiers jumped out and ran toward him. They tossed him into one of the vans and drove away. The arrest, they told him, served as a lesson to other persons willing to defy the government's laws. There would be no publications without the express permission of the government.

The army raided the meeting house, arresting one man from the meeting and releasing the other. They also arrested the owners of the building and their associates. The imprisonment of these high-ranking businessmen who were known opposition to the government was popular with supporters of the ruling party but not with international organizations.

Victor's group was the largest and most effective known opposition to the government. Its challenge to the government had provoked concern in the region, and its link to the CIA complicated life for Victor in prison.

At that time, the then-prime minister came on the radio to explain the arrest of Victor and the others, whom he called monsters. He said they gave the government no choice but to shut them down before they festered and became more aggressive and widespread.

In prison, Victor and his group held courage and met to reaffirm their opposition to the government and to plan their own democracy. In footage smuggled from behind bars, Victor and his group are showing the victory sign with their fingers.

The arrest propelled Victor and the others to international stardom. They were fighters for democracy and international justice. This positioned Victor to form the MDM and enter mainstream politics.

Mabuya's deep recession was compounded by the government's unpopular decision to detain political prisoners without a trial. This action cost Mabuya lots of developmental aid and low-interest financing. The government was unable to meet basic daily needs.

This policy was a major reason for the government's fall and Karl Stone's rise to power. Karl came to power promising the world. He had an answer to every problem faced by the nation. Victor and his cohorts had been in prison for two years and six months when Karl Stone came to power. One day the commissioner of prisons visited them and said they were free to go home.

Victor looks over at Allyson, who is sound asleep. He turns away and thinks of his plans for the next day.

***

Michelle Stone is on the phone with Diana James.

"Yeah, he in the bathroom getting ready to go," she says. "Every night he is after a woman. He will contract a disease."

"Do you know where he is going tonight?" Diana asks.

"To a stinking bitch who has no respect for people's marriage. I don't care which one."

"Why don't you stop it?" Diana asks.

"Girlfriend, I am too old for this. I will be sixty-eight in September. Let this man run

himself into the ground if he so desires."

"One of these days, you will have to stop him."

Michelle removes her wig and places it on the bed stand.

"Maybe I should do something different with my hair?"

"That might help."

"But changing my style at my age?"

"You might turn him on. Do something."

"I am lost."

"You need to relax. Be less official in your approach."

Michelle knows she is a perfectionist, unbending. She and Kenny have more in common than she and Karl. She and Kenny both have high moral standards for themselves and others, but she also has an issue with self-control and repressed anger.

"Girl, this is easy to say."

"You cannot always stay the same way."

"In the beginning, I used to try. I bought every sexy negligee there was. I would put them on and parade in front of him. He would scoff at me and leave."

"Did he ever love you?"

"Maybe not."

"Put another way, is he capable of love?"

"That is another serious question."

"Not every man can love."

"True."

"Girlfriend, you need to find answers. This guy married you."

"For forty years."

"And you don't know him?"

"Diana, I am committed to the marriage. I said 'I do' before God."

"Only you can talk about your complications, baby."

"Girl, you remember when we were doing our bachelor's degree, Karl could barely pay for his classes. A stressed-out student living on a student loan, he claimed. Later, we found out he had lied. He had stolen the money from his workplace and ran away from his country."

"Rescued by your parents' money."

"Girl, my father was so upset. He didn't send me to university to pick up men. As a matter of fact, a poverty-stricken, dishonest man."

"Michelle, your father didn't understand how desperate and relentless Karl was."

"I also. This was my first contact with a man so determined to get what he is after."

"It was a stark contrast. Our parents had provided for us to finance our way through the four years. On the contrary, here was a penniless man deciding he will sponge his way through."

"And succeeded."

"Fortunately, he didn't pull you down into his depressive state."

"Impossible. We were young and vibrant."

"Remember, too, these boys on campus were always fussing and worried about their success, while we were relaxed and confident. Others turned to drugs, alcohol or dropped out in the first year. We carried on."

"Karl was eager to succeed. He wanted desperately to impress. As far as he was concerned, he was born to lead. Never to follow. He said he would be the prime minister of his country one day, and I must decide if I wanted to be the wife of a prime minister."

"He needed you."

"I taught him how to cope. We got married quietly, deciding we would have a bigger event when we left university and had our own money. My father treated him like a son. The son he never had."

"Your family rescued him."

"He is coming out of the bathroom. I'll talk to you."

"Okay."

Michelle picks back up her Bible and opens it. She surveys Karl as he strides out of the bathroom with a towel around his waist. This is not the man she fell in love with at university. The man she met was aspiring for greatness. His main goal at the time was to get his doctorate. He was a catch—unmarried, no children. He loved sports but didn't want to be just a player on the team; he wanted to lead. Signs of his duplicity began when she realized that though he had grown up as a working-class youth on Mabuya, he had a deep hatred for his working-class roots. She learned there was nothing stopping him from getting what he wanted.

His personality changed when people started calling him "Doc." At last he had arrived; he was now part of the elite class he had always admired.

Her eyes follow him as he dresses and leaves the room.

Michelle reflects on when she felt that Karl's morality and rationality started deteriorating; he had agreed to become a CIA agent. They financed his campaign to win a seat in parliament and later funded his challenge to the leader of the MNP. That year he won the leadership of the party but lost the election for prime minister of the country.

He went into a frenzy, spending the next five years reorganizing the party and developing a formidable force for the next election. His victory has had him in power for the past fifteen years, twenty in parliament.

When his obsession with power and money hoarding began, Michelle saw him lose his faith, philosophy, his allegiance to his country and commitment to others. He has no gratitude to anyone, except for his mother.

He became a fitness fanatic and developed a hatred for anyone who wasn't, including Michelle. She had tried to keep up with him, until she realized that it was not her passion, not her life. In her research, she found that Karl suffered from bigorexia. The condition, also called muscle dysmorphia, is an anxiety disorder that causes someone to see themselves as small, unfit, and too fat despite being firm and muscular. The research shows one in ten men training in gyms may have the condition, which can lead to depression, feelings of inadequacy, and rage.

It is a form of reverse anorexia. The constant pressure to join him in training has affected her. Her body is always too old and soft for him. She lives under the constant pressure to become muscular and hard.

Over the years he has forced her to understand his extreme concern with his body and appearance. He counters his depression by hunting women.

Michelle often wonders why. She links his agitation to his quest for power and authority. His urge for success, dominance, and appeal masks his low self-esteem and anxiety.

From her research, she learned that the condition can be genetic or arise from a chemical imbalance in the brain. It is common in people who had a frustrated childhood.

She chuckles to herself as she realizes that apart from his unpredictable temperament being one among the long list of side effects, there is also his hair loss and testicle shrinkage.

What hurt her the most was when young women started praising his physique and sexual prowess in her presence. He reveled in the admiration. Michelle was no match for the vulnerable women he preyed upon. They wanted his money, to feel his power, and he discarded them as quickly as he used them.

She hears the gate swing open. A teardrop falls on her Bible. Karl is gone.

She dabs her eyes with a rag and continues to read.

***

Diana cuts her conversation short when she hears a knock at the door. She hangs up the phone, looks through the window, and opens the door to let Karl in.

He's wearing sporty shorts, a flowered shirt, leather slippers, and a cap pulled over his head.

"How many times ah tell you that people could still make you out in that cap." Diana laughs.

"Baby, love does not worry who says what," Karl responds. "When a man is in love, he follows the pussy."

"Oh, you got pussy on your mind," Diana teases.

"My time is short." He is abrupt.

"As usual."

Karl flicks off his slippers and unbuttons his shirt.

"Poor timing, brother. It is that time of the month."

"So, why you let me come?"

"You didn't tell me you were coming. Your wife told me you were going somewhere. She didn't know where."

"That bitch called you?"

"She is your wife. Don't call her a bitch."

"What you want me to call her?"

"You would like nobody to call your mother a bitch or a witch."

"Leave my mother out of this." Karl buttons up his shirt and puts his slippers back on. "If you want our relationship to continue, never you compare my mother with that bitch I married."

Diana looks on as Karl struts out to the yard. He climbs into an old Toyota Corolla and speeds off into the night.

"What an asshole," she mutters and makes the sign of the cross. "Heaven forgive me."

She closes her door and picks up the phone.

Within minutes she hears the roar of the motorbike. She peels back the window blinds to see Richard climb off the Harley-Davidson cruiser, run up the stairs, and walk through her open front door.

"You sure he's not coming back?" Richard asks.

"Positive," Diana says. "He never has time. His attention span is short. He is processing the next thing he must do. Most likely, jogging in the morning."

He removes his helmet and riding suit, kicking them to one side. He stands naked before her.

She drops her gown to expose her sleepwear and walks into Richard's arms. They hug and kiss.

"Why do you need him?"

"I don't. But he serves a purpose."

"This is a situation you no longer need. With your status in life you can move on and live comfortably, but you continue to allow this."

"I have a plan. I need to achieve a level of independence and authority before dumping him."

"Just leave him."

"You don't know this guy. I can't just leave him."

"I am here."

"Don't even go there. It's your fault I even work for him—you're the one who assigned me to him."

"I know." Richard bows his head.

She takes him by the hand and leads him into the bedroom. They sit on the bed, and she cuddles in his lap.

"He still thinks I am this vulnerable woman he preyed upon so many years ago."

"Are you?"

"Don't be foolish, Richard."

"Darling, I accept responsibility. This was the way to get to him."

"I knew the risks."

"We didn't expect him to latch on."

"Richard, this man is a child. He preys upon unsuspecting women. Although he has had his fair share of women in his youth, he is never satisfied."

"He has a wife for Christ's sake."

"He regrets his marriage since it prevents him from having more women, but on the other hand, his wife is a convenience. She's there for public presentations and shielding him from awkward situations."

"Poor sucker."

"Every time I say I am done, he goes into a frenzy. He fears he might lose control over me and becomes obsessive."

"That is dangerous. I will have to pull you out."

"He is this great cult leader, rallying weak women against an unknown evil. Every day he draws in another. They love his shit talk. Once they are in, he uses the political party machinery to help them with favors and to win their friends and relatives."

"I will talk to Control. Seriously, it's time to pull you out."

She breaks away from him and says, "I know just what you need."

"Just think about it."

"Stay here and relax. I will call you when I'm ready."

"I'll be here." Richard relents, reclining on the bed as Diana goes to the bathroom.

In the bathroom, she glimpses herself in the mirror. *Richard is right,* she thinks. *Time to turn a new page, open a new chapter, even start a different book.* She runs both pipes in the Jacuzzi and drops some fragrant essential oils into the tub.

As her handler, Richard has used her to collect information from Mabuya and to keep an eye on Karl's activities. As her lover, she finds him fit and intelligent.

Over the years, she learned that he was an asset to the United States intelligence services, versatile with languages and adaptable among people—a loyal American who defends foreign policy without question.

He believes in his country's ideals, such as justice and freedom, and he will die for them.

Her taught her to think but not outside the ideals of the organization. She learned never to challenge the establishment or harbor her own ideas about how a country should be governed. When in doubt, he instructed her to check the service manual.

She lights some candles around the tub, watching their flames cast flickering shadows around the room.

"Done some remodeling, I see," Richard says from the doorway.

"I said I'd call you. You've ruined the surprise," she says.

They admire the new additions: storage shelves for stacking toilet paper, extra makeup, rags and towels. A new shower flowing off on a sharp gradient. Exquisite his and hers smoky glass sinks diffuse the recessed lights throughout the room.

Through the window, the soft moonlight brightens Diana's face, and Richard looks at her as if they are at the beginning of their courtship. For him, each time is the first time. He believes that, over time, people in intimate relationships earn success, acceptance, and love through constant performance.

For him, image is everything, to the point of deceiving himself about his true feelings. He is always trying to show his intense concern for her. She tries to show him their love is real, but he thinks it must be groomed.

"Well done," he says.

"I knew you would love it. It's roomier."

He steps into the Jacuzzi, and she switches on the bubbles.

Richard leans back and closes his eyes. Diana playfully throws water and bubbles on his chest.

CHAPTER FOUR

Four men are jogging along a remote road in the countryside of Mabuya. One man runs marginally ahead; the others run abreast of Karl in the middle. They jog at a steady pace, keeping their formation in the flats, uphill and downhill. A few meters to the rear, a black SUV trails along, never too close or too far from them.

They follow the road into the valley, across the farmlands and into the suburbs. They jog alongside the river into a municipal called Riverdale. Their feet bounce in and out of potholes along the road as old as its name: the Caribe, named by Indigenous people who occupied Mabuya before the arrival of Europeans. The runners make better progress as the road gets smoother.

They turn onto gravel roads every few meters, making traction difficult. The compensation is the lack of cars and trucks, no noise but the rushing wind. Old quarter-mile markers along the way allow the runners to gauge their progress. The trail takes a serpentine course through the valley before bringing them onto a road with heavy vehicular traffic.

On the roadside are vendor booths designed for locals to showcase their products to tourists. Off to one side, a single two-story building has historical displays and public restrooms. The trail turns into a tarmac road, popular among cyclists with hybrid bikes and fatter tires.

This part of the island connects the suburbs to the town center. The men take the road to the city, their sneakers squeaking on the asphalt.

After skirting the southern edge of the city, they cross the river bridge and turn toward home.

The route takes them past the soccer and cricket fields. They lose cover of the trees along this stretch. The road becomes solid concrete, increasing the slapping sound from their shoes. Windows open as people wake up and look outside. Other joggers run in the opposite direction.

Suddenly, a huge truck comes around a corner and heads straight for the group. The security men respond, grabbing Karl and pulling him off to one side as the truck hisses, speeds around the corner, and disappears.

"Boss, we have to abandon this one," a security officer says.

"I agree." Karl is breathless.

They signal to the driver of the SUV, and he pulls up. Karl gets in and they abandon their morning run.

***

Karl is pacing around his office talking on his cellphone. The three clocks on the wall show different times, one for London, one for China, and one for the Caribbean. The Caribbean clock shows six forty-five.

The door opens and a young female security guard enters.

"Good morning, prime minister," she greets him.

"Good morning, young lady." Karl lowers the cell phone.

"What can I do for you, sir?" she asks.

"Set up the coffee machine."

"I am on it."

Karl returns to his conversation, while the guard fiddles with the cof-fee machine. After a moment, he gets off the phone to stare at the curvaceous ass of the young guard. She purposely wiggles her backside while she works.

Karl shakes his head as if to change his vision; still, he licks his lips at the tempting sight. The woman turns and catches Karl drooling.

He recovers, straightens himself, and restores his officious look.

"No need to be embarrassed, sir. I know I look good." She smiles.

"You caught me. I surrender."

"You can see the real thing. Any time you ready."

"I am always ready."

The guard controls her shock. "Here? Now?"

"Why not?"

"You're the boss."

Coffee forgotten, she drops her trousers to show a bright red thong and a dark, smooth, curvy ass. Karl wastes no time. He drops his trousers and mounts her backside in a flash.

The affair ends as quickly as it started. Before the second hand of the clock can make its revolution, Karl backs away, wipes his penis with his handkerchief, and fixes his trousers. The guard straightens her thong and pulls her trousers back up.

She looks at him.

Karl is apologetic. "That was quick. Normally I am able to last longer."

She smiles and pecks him on the cheek.

"There is more," she says. "I am always around, sir."

"I...I will hold you to it," he stutters.

The guard slithers toward the door and blows a kiss at Karl before she leaves. He walks around to his high-backed chair and slumps into it. As his conquest closes the door behind her, Karl looks to the heavens.

"God. How am I supposed to focus on my work today?" he mutters.

There is a knock on the door.

"Come in!" he shouts.

Swaggart enters the office.

"Boss, we were able to track the guy from this morning."

Karl sits up, suddenly alert.

"And..."

"It is the Rasta from the bar in Caress."

"Somebody gave him a truck to drive?"

"It's a government truck."

"Which ministry?" Karl snarls at Swaggart.

"Agriculture."

"Well, you know what to do."

"I am on it."

Swaggart turns to leave the room.

"And Swaggart..."

Swaggart spins around. "Yes, boss."

"The female security guard outside, make sure she is on the list for the housing program."

"No problem, boss."

Swaggart leaves the room.

***

Karl straightens his tie and settles himself in his seat at the head of the oval table in the Cabinet room. On one side of the table sit Jules Bourne and Ingrid Frank. Diana James and Colonel Lester Bynoe are on the other side. Cathy Gordon, the Cabinet secretary, sits separately at a desk away from the members.

"We will start with a word of prayer," Karl announces.

Pastor Providence, of the Holy Apostle Church, enters the room.

Karl stands and beckons the others to follow. They stand.

Pastor begins, "Lord we ask for your guidance as we deliberate today on the weighty matters of the state of Mabuya. Lord, we know that our country is small, but the responsibility placed on our shoulders is huge.

"Lord, we pray for our leader. May he continue to have health and strength. We ask that you fill him with wisdom and knowledge to make the right decisions. Lord, we ask for protection from evil and from his enemies.

"Cast them away, Lord. Deliver him from the hands of the devil, from the hands of iniquity. We pray this in Jesus's name and in the name of the Holy Spirit. Amen."

The pastor bows and exits the room.

Karl sits and everyone follows.

"Diana, why were your eyes open?" Karl asks.

"I am not a hypocrite," Diana says with no emotion.

Cathy shuffles her papers and clears her throat. Karl flashes her a grimace.

He looks at his agenda, avoiding a confrontation with Diana.

"Members," he starts, "the first matter comes from the Ministry of Finance. This is a proposal for the review of the Customs Department. This was not cleared with me."

"I signed it when you were out," Jules explains.

"These items should not come before Cabinet without me seeing them," Karl informs him. "No matter where I am. Stand this aside for review.

"The second matter is again from finance, a proposal to buy a vehicle for the Planning Unit. I saw that and approved it.

"The third document is a proposal from the Ministry of Agriculture, for government investment in a pig farm in the Highlands."

Karl turns to Jules. Jules, who had been muttering something to Ingrid, turns his attention back to Karl.

"You approved this?"

"It is a proposal developed by the technicians in the ministry."

"So, up to now the technicians in the ministry are not aware of government policy?"

"They know, but they believe that there can be exceptions."

"Why?"

"The proposal is part of a holistic approach to enhance the region, increase production, and reduce poverty."

"That cannot override the basic government policy not to get involved in matters where the private sector can do it better. Also, as a fundamental principle, this country will not be developed by investing in agriculture. Why can't they get that through their thick skulls?"

"Okay." Jules shakes his head.

The other members of the Cabinet exchange glances.

"Disapproved." Karl angrily slides the document away from him. "Let's move on. The final matter for consideration is the new hospital and the awarding of the contract for construction. We have the report from the Tenders Board for the approval of the Cabinet.

"Cathy, you and I will meet separately on this. Ladies and gentlemen, thank you for coming. There is lunch, but I cannot stay. I have a few outstanding matters to catch up with. Enjoy the lunch. I'll see you guys."

Karl stands and exits the room.

***

Diana remains sitting at the table after Karl and the other members leave. Colonel Bynoe walks over and joins her.

"At the risk of being sexist, you look as bootylicious as ever," he says.

"Colonel, I am shocked," she retorts. "Didn't know you knew that word."

"I am of the world, Diana," he claims.

Diana analyzes his clothes. She notes that he hates colonial suits and prefers to dress in Nehru collar linen or cotton shirts and plain-colored trousers or jeans.

"You sure are of this world, Colonel."

She studies him—dark eyes making him look older than his forty-five years. His five-foot-seven, stocky build matches the clean-shaven, close-cropped black hair peppered with a few strands of gray. He rubs his temple.

"That was a sharp exchange, Diana," he says.

"I am coming to the end of my tether with this guy." She pounds her fist in her palm.

"Don't bother with him. Consider the country," the colonel says softly.

"Colonel, I am not sure where that will get me," she protests.

"You might stay poor, Diana, but you keep your dignity."

"Colonel, it sounds cliché, but many patriots die penniless and without recognition. At the funeral everyone says how great they were and salutes their contribution to the country. Within days, it all fades away, while they bury the next fallen hero."

"But they die with their dignity."

"Can dignity put food on the table? The most concrete attempts at immortality all crumble in the end. New rulers tear down the statues of old relics, erasing them from history. With one bulldozer and a chain, they erase hundreds of years of history."

"Diana, you are sounding mercenary."

"Maybe I am. I have to be. As a woman in a world of men, I am a dolphin surrounded by great white sharks. I am alive because they allow me to be. I forget the basis of my existence to my peril."

"I disagree. I see you as a pillar of strength. A Julie mango in an orchard of Lung mango. One bright star, shining through a faded cluster," he states.

"I do not expect you to understand. You are a man, and in addition, Karl has always treated you differently. With respect and dignity. I don't know what hold you have on him, but he deals with you respectfully. He listens to your advice and carries it out."

"Only on matters of state."

"That is not what everybody thinks."

"They can think whatever they want."

"Colonel, people say you advise him on everything. They believe you are responsible for all his actions, particularly among women. How does a wife-loving, churchgoing mother's boy transform into a womanizing, adulterous rude boy after teaming up with you?" she asks.

"Are you accusing me?" he asks.

"I want to know."

"Can't help you."

"What do you guys talk about when you are finished discussing politics?"

"Sports."

"Never women?"

"Never." He is adamant.

She likes the colonel's friendly character. He associates with everyone and does not distinguish based on class. He enjoys discussing calypsos and is a walking encyclopedia on the music. Mention the Mighty Sparrow, Calypso king of the world, and he keeps you in conversation for the next hour on the exploits of the man.

He is self-disciplined and principled, emotionally controlled. He believes there is one path in life—the right path.

"Colonel Bynoe, I don't think you fully understand how devious our leader can be."

"I concede."

"You are not dealing with a fully evolved human being here."

"I hear you."

"Not everything can be rationalized. Everyone does not act reasonably."

"Agreed."

"Be careful how you exercise your reasonableness, Colonel. People do not act correctly every time. You will not always have a perfect outcome. but you can exercise self-control and avoid making mistakes. Not everyone thinks that way. You will learn."

The colonel recalls the first election campaign. He and Karl met at the end of every day to discuss their progress. Later, Karl admitted to him that he could not sleep without assessing their daily performance.

The ruling party at the time had allowed the election period to expire beyond the constitutional due date. The island was emerging from a period of economic structural adjustment. The daily hardship faced by the ordinary man became a main topic in the months before the election date was announced.

Bynoe and Karl fought over the theme of his campaign. Karl wanted to focus on his ideas for infrastructural development of the island. The colonel insisted that he attack the economy under structural development with examples of the MNP doing better for the people of the country.

Gradually, Karl accepted Colonel Bynoe's strategy and began focusing on the economy at his public meetings, attacking the ruling party and convincing his minions that his own party would perform differently. He called for a breaking down of the divisions between the supporters of the style of politics the country was used to in which promises were made at election time only to broken.

Another difference in opinion developed when Bynoe disagreed with Karl's insistence on using members of the Mfeka Labor Party (MLP) from Mfeka Island and his friendship with Walid Agar, the leader of the party. Walid Agar and the MLP were successful in convincing the working people to destroy their organizations while promoting themselves as the solution to all the country's problems.

Walid Agar was linked to a massacre of twelve innocent men in an area of his country called Orange Bay. Eyewitnesses saw the young men idling in the area, smoking, drinking, and playing music. The army approached the men in search of one suspect who may or may not have been a part of the group. Walid, as minister of defense in the government, instructed the army to kill them all.

During sixty years in politics on Mfeka Island, Walid Agar developed a structure of an extrajudicial "posse," which openly promoted violence against the opposition. The posse raised millions of dollars from the drug trade and as a beneficiary run by the CIA to promote division in the islands.

Colonel Bynoe had to resist the temptation put forward by these advisers to rely on their strategy from Mfeka to destroy the hope, dignity, and values of the opposition, at the same time, promoting gang warfare as a means of succeeding in politics.

At a meeting one night, they'd argued until they saw the sun rising in the east. The colonel realized that Karl was all mouth and no cojones. He was a wannabe CIA agent willing to hide behind Ollie North's and Walid

Agar's actions but was not willing to set up the drug posse and death squads needed to carry out the acts.

To Colonel Bynoe, Walid Agar was a man of fluid ideological conviction. Karl was a supporter of Walid Agar, who opposed the Cuban Revolution and its political outlook, yet he accepted Cuban scholarships and sent students to Cuba to study. He also accepted Cuban professionals coming to Mabuya Island to work.

Karl's support for Agar's policies did not extend to the setting up of sweatshops for the exploitation of the people of his country. The colonel realized this was not by choice but because Karl knew the people of Mabuya would not accept this as a way of life.

When cornered, Karl takes refuge in academia. He reminds everyone of his PhD and his membership in the elite fellowships at universities in Florida and Texas.

"Are you sure you should be telling me this?" Diana asks Colonel Bynoe.

"No one has ever accused you of lack of confidentiality. This discussion will stay between us."

They look at each other in quiet agreement.

***

Karl is standing at his office window observing the scenery and vegetation outside. His eyes move from the Ministry of Finance on the compound to the Ministry of Education off in the distance.

He had wanted the ministries to be in one complex. However, upon construction, he realized the current building was too small to accommodate everyone. The builders had adjusted the plan without consulting him—an affront to his authority.

His vision was to ensure workers' comfort with their surroundings, improving productivity in the workplace. He wanted the place to have a striking and dramatic effect on personnel.

To accomplish this, he asked the architects and contractors to apply modern life-cycle analysis and use an integrated design approach. This was meant to create a high-performance office building to improve workers' health and create greater flexibility, heightened energy, and environmental performance.

Besides durable and aesthetically pleasing architecture, the comfort of the workers was paramount. He'd requested that the contractors augment initial investments in architectural design, systems selection, and building construction.

Karl did not get what he wanted.

So, he made sure detailed attention was paid to the selection of interior finishes and installations in entry spaces, conference rooms, and other areas with public access.

The knock on the door brings him back to reality.

"It's open!" he yells.

Cathy enters carrying a pile of files. He looks at her questioningly.

"Where are you going with this load?"

"I thought we had to meet."

"Oh, the contract!" He grins. "Give it to the Canadian company."

"Prime minister, do you think this is the correct way?"

"What do you mean?"

"You might want to reconsider your approach, knowing that you signed on to abide by anti-money-laundering and anti-corruption laws."

"Signing the laws does not mean I lose my independence and decision-making ability."

"What it gives you is responsibility, sir. You are required to lead the march against illegal acts. You are the one granting to drive compliance; the prime minister needs an active program showing commitment to the morals and ethics expected of his position."

"Are you accusing me of corruption?"

"No, prime minister, not at all." Cathy freezes with the bundle cradled in her arms.

"What else?" he asks.

"No, no, no...no, that's fine," Cathy stutters.

She turns to leave the room.

"Ask Jules to see me."

Karl resumes staring out the window.

Jules Bourne walks in without knocking.

"Have a seat, Jules," Karl says without looking around. "How are the development programs going?"

"We are on track to finish our quota for the year."

Karl stares at Jules. The fifty-one-year-old is Karl's natural successor as leader of the MNP and prime minister of Mabuya.

Jules's effectiveness is without question. Karl knows Jules to be a team player, a man who believes the team is counting on his role to fulfill the plan. The weakness in his approach is that he doesn't always consider other team members. He relies heavily on his ability to control them, steamrolling and overpowering them—with Karl's support.

"Do you have the resources you need?" Karl asks.

"Enough," says Jules.

"You will have to double up."

"I am ready."

"Get your forces together. Get ready for the election."

"Election?"

"Yes. Soon."

"I am on it."

"You know the drill. Roll it out."

"I will take care of it. What date are we working with?"

This is where Karl draws the line. Over the years, he has learned never to divulge too much information. His modus operandi is control—control others with the use of information. They must wait until he offers measured doses of data like drips from an intravenous solution.

Despite their closeness, Karl didn't view Jules as his successor. He gives him specific tasks to perform, limits his information, and forces him to always come back for further instructions. For Karl, this relationship works since Jules doesn't have to make his own decisions. He relies on Karl to do the thinking for him. Karl is aware of Jules's resistance to control and dependence; however, he ignores the changes in Jules's moods.

"I haven't decided yet."

"Let me know."

Jules leaves the office.

CHAPTER FIVE

Milosevic is sitting on the passenger side of the all-terrain vehicle (ATV) as the driver picks his way through the abandoned sugarcane plantation with Karl's ATV in tow. Behind Karl and his security detail, Jules and his driver struggle to maintain the pace.

The Mountain Drew Estate has been grown over by a mixture of native and exotic scrubs. They drive under a canopy of scrubs, finding tracks left by cane haulers over the previous decades. On the steeper slopes, they travel under taller trees, which give way to open pastures intermittently.

At the top of a hill, in an open pasture, Milosevic's driver pulls over and stops. He crawls out of the vehicle and signals the others to follow him. He waves his hand over the valley on the opposite side as the scrubs give way to mangrove and swampland. In the distance a white sand beach is tucked away between two marine protected areas and a national park.

"This is what I am talking about, gentlemen," he says. "Nowhere else in the world can you get this view."

"This is my first time here," Karl notes.

"I used to come to the estate as a child to harvest sugarcane," Jules says. "I have never seen this view."

"A gem." Milosevic is proud. "Look around where we stand, gentlemen. What do you see?"

The men look around with blank faces.

"We are standing among the ruins of the old Mountain Drew Estate great house." Milosevic explains. "During the site preparation phase of this project, we plan to restore the great house. It will be a replica of the old one."

"That will shut up those environmentalists." Karl rubs his hands together.

"Prime minister, we intend to preserve the ecology of this area," Milosevic tells him. "We are ahead of the environmentalists. Our plans exceed the requirements of the environmental impact assessment."

"I realize that," Jules says.

"See those two ponds down there?" Milosevic points to two bodies of water at the side of the mangrove. "They are essential for shorebirds and seabirds. We will enhance these ponds, making it better for the birds."

"Show us the layout of the project," Karl responds.

"Let us drive to the other side of this hill. This is where the project comes to life," Milosevic says and walks to his vehicle.

They return to the ATVs and descend the hill. They drive past the remnants of a pig farm and goat pens. The government once used the estate as an experimental farm where the best breeds were cultivated and used to maintain the breed quality.

When Karl came to power, he closed the farm based on his philosophy that government should not be involved in business. He saw the farm as a private sector activity and a drain on the consolidated fund.

Cattle and sheep still graze along the roadside as they drive by. Villagers from nearby use the uninhabited area to rear the animals for personal consumption.

They drive past areas where farmers squat to produce sugarcane, watermelons, cantaloupe, squash, cucumbers, sweet potatoes, pumpkins, okra, and sorrel, on plots averaging one to two acres.

Milosevic's ATV pulls up in another clear area overlooking a bay and an island in the distance. Karl and his entourage follow.

"This is where the action takes place." Milosevic points to where the gently sloping hill merges with a black sand beach and the channel to the island. "We will build a bridge to connect the island with the mainland. This will be done in the preliminary stage of the project."

"The next time we come here, we will be driving across." Karl smiles at Milosevic.

"In fine style," Milosevic continues. "The eighteen-hole golf course will run along this ridge through the natural ponds and over the soggy ground. The seventy-room hotel will be close to the waterfront and the beach. We will distribute 220 villas along the ridge for private residences. On the island, we will have a marina and entertainment facilities including fine dining restaurants."

"You will need special permission to build and develop lands in a national park," Jules announces.

"I will take care of that," Karl states bluntly.

"What do you think, prime minister?" Milosevic asks.

"It's approved," Karl says.

"Cabinet will decide," Jules says.

"Of course." Karl is sarcastic.

Milosevic returns to his ATV and signals the driver forward. They follow Milosevic's ATV into the scrubs.

***

Victor pulls into the car park across the road from the US Embassy on Mabuya Island. He exits the car and looks across the road at the fortified building. Though there had been no security breaches on the island, with every new instruction from Washington, the embassy regularly adds another layer of security—the US government's stipulations for minimum security at its overseas postings.

Since vehicles are not allowed within a certain range of the embassy building, Victor crosses the road and walks toward the thick reinforced wall with added barbed wire fencing at the top. The guard stops him for his first inspection. He informs her of his appointment with Richard South, and she waves him in.

He walks through the body scanner and meets Richard on the other side. The tall, lanky man leads the way through the building, up the stairs to the first floor, through a short corridor, and into his office.

"What's your poison?" Richard asks. "Coffee?"

"Nah. Water will do," Victor says.

Richard presses the phone intercom and places the order—coffee for himself. He lounges back in the chair as Victor takes a seat.

Victor lowers himself into the chair and notes the sign on Richard's desk: *United States Defense Attaché*. Richard's office comes under the secretary of defense and the Joint Chiefs of Staff.

"Great to see you again, Vic," Richard says. "You are looking good."

"You look as sharp as ever." Victor is uneasy around Richard. He remembers the first time they met. Richard was a combat soldier in full military uniform and assigned to train officers on Mabuya Island. As the leader of the opposition, Victor had attended the passing out parade held at the camp.

Every parade, each ceremony is unique. Proud family and friends witness the new recruits graduating from training and entering the ranks of the police force. Among those passing out on each occasion are new high school and college graduates plus those who had abandoned former careers to enter the police force. This year there is a former nurse, an assistant accountant, and a barman.

After completion of the twenty-week training course and the parade and ceremony, new recruits are posted across the island to protect and serve. Being their trainer was Richard's introduction to law enforcement on Mabuya.

Before coming to Mabuya and with years of criminal investigative experience and an excellent performance record, Richard had completed the Criminal Investigator Training Program at the Federal Law Enforcement Training Center before joining the Foreign Service for diplomatic training.

"Wondering why I called you here?" Richard asks Victor.

As an undercover agent, Richard worked alone and blossomed under pressure. Rumor had it that he could gather and assimilate large quantities of data, analyze the key issues, and draw suitable conclusions.

"Tell me," Victor answers.

He wonders what Richard has gleaned from interacting with the wide range of people he meets daily. Does he use sound judgment to elicit information in difficult and sensitive circumstances? Obviously, his rise in rank was due to his skill in negotiation, tact, discretion, and diplomacy, but Victor hasn't figured out how Richard remains cool and friendly.

"Get ready to be the next prime minister."

"Why?"

Richard's assistant knocks and enters the room with the drinks. He tests his coffee and signals his satisfaction.

"Karl is approaching the end of the line," he tells Victor after dismissing the assistant.

"I thought he was your man?"

"Not anymore. He is not listening."

"What makes you think I will listen?"

"We will have to see."

"What happened with Karl?"

"This man is an embarrassment. He has no conscience and owes allegiance to no one. He enjoys crooked business transactions. Con artist after con artist flood this country with their vile ways, and he tolerates and encourages them."

"You will not be supporting him in the next elections?"

"No."

"Have you told him that?"

"I am telling you first. Get yourself ready. I am giving you a head start."

"Appreciated." Victor sips his water.

Richard stands and walks to the window.

"This country deserves a break," he says.

"I agree," Victor responds.

"After training your men in the armed forces, I begged to stay here. It was the closest thing to paradise on earth."

"Thank you for the information." Victor stands to leave.

"One more thing." Richard extends a handshake to Victor. "We will expose him soon. Look out for it. This will signal the end of our relationship with him."

"Great." Victor shakes Richard's hand and finishes his water before Richard escorts him out of the office.

"In the meantime, keep your eyes on your general secretary, Aadesh," Richard whispers in Victor's ear. "Don't let him surprise you."

"Tell me what you know, my friend." Victor pleads.

"Watch him," Richard states.

***

A white Toyota Corolla with tinted windows pulls up outside the Royal Mabuyan Hotel lobby. Karl steps out and enters the hotel.

Swaggart takes the car around to the car park.

Karl strides up to the smiling young woman at the front desk.

"There is a room reserved for me."

"Yes, sir."

She retrieves the key and hands it over to Karl.

"Enjoy your stay with us, sir." She smiles.

"Thanks," says Karl. "My driver will follow."

"That will be fine, sir. If you need me, call. We aim to please."

Karl peels himself away from the receptionist to find Swaggart standing behind him. He hands the key to Swaggart, and they walk along the hallway to the room. Swaggart unlocks the door, while Karl remains by the doorway. Swaggart goes in and does a security sweep. With the way clear, Karl enters.

Once inside, Karl hangs up his jacket and loosens his tie. The hotel room is a luxurious double suite. A small archway leads to a king-sized master bedroom. Swaggart takes up a position toward the far end of the kitchenette and reads a travel booklet from the magazine rack.

Karl opens a bottle of water and pours himself a glass.

"Think they will be long?" Karl asks.

"I hope not, boss," Swaggart says.

"They should be here." Karl swears. "They had better bring my shit!"

"You will be fine, boss," Swaggart reassures him. "They look like nice people."

Karl paces the room.

The door inside the adjoining bedroom opens, and a dark, leggy blond woman comes out. Her open robe reveals a pair of firm bare breasts; a flat, hard stomach; and a fluorescent green thong. Karl guesses her roasted dark skin is from recent overexposure to the sun, or a sunbed.

"Mr. Milosevic will see you now," she says. "Please follow me."

Karl leaves Swaggart and follows her into the next suite.

Andre Milosevic is in his boxers near the open sliding door leading to the balcony. Milosevic is a pale Slovak man who lives well. His soft milky fingers curl around a lit cigar. Even with his back turned, Karl can see the extra folds of Milosevic's waistline spilling out on both sides of his boxers.

Milosevic turns as Karl brazenly eyes the open briefcase with United States currency lying on the bed.

"It's there," Milosevic says, pointing at the money. "Just as you requested."

Karl closes the briefcase and lifts it.

Milosevic stabs out the cigar in the ashtray and looks Karl in the eye.

"When do I get the license?" he asks.

"Within days," Karl assures. "I will set things in motion as soon as I leave here."

"Great. We agree then."

Karl steals another quick look at the blond woman.

"Bye."

"See you, Karl," she whispers.

Karl drags himself out of the room.

***

Victor walks into the restaurant to meet newspaper editor Errol Bullen, who is sitting at a table for two by the water side. Errol stands as Victor approaches. They greet each other, then sit.

"The election campaign tempo is heating up." Errol laughs.

"Too fast for me," Victor says.

"It's never too fast. Keep up with it, man. Every election campaign has a life of its own. It starts slowly, then creeps up on you."

"This is my life, Errol. I have spent fifty years in this business. People say I will die without being the prime minister. I am not in this for fame.

I want to see our people protected and their constitutional rights safe-guarded."

"Errol, at this time you maintain your health and strength and keep your party on message. In the run-up to elections, there is a danger of peaking too early. One prime minister became frustrated by the process and turned to alcohol. His operatives would find him drunk or sleeping every time they reported to him.

"The ruling party has to show restraint. Not too much bluffing. They should not overspend. After boasting of lighting the national stadium, building a new hospital, and constructing highways, a party felt it was on the way to a landslide victory, only to lose the whole damn election. Voters were turned off by the spending and the boasting."

Victor responds, "Karl had the advantage; he knew the date long before we did. It's like having a head start in a race. He began spending and pumped up his people long before he announced the date. He launched his campaign, then announced the date of the election."

"There was a prime minister who called the election date while none of his candidates were ready."

"The poor man had to be scrambling for candidates during the campaign."

"I ordered," says Errol. "Grilled fish with sautéed potatoes and vegetables. What do you want?"

"Same," Victor says. "At our age, I don't think we can eat anything else."

"Funny, when we were young and could eat a horse, we ended up in prison eating bread and porridge. Now we have the food available to us and we can't eat." A waitress takes Victor's order.

"Any drinks, gentlemen?" she asks.

"Scotch on the rocks for me," Errol requests.

"I will stick to water," says Victor.

"Wise choice," Errol chimes in.

Victor looks at his longtime friend and partner in crime. At sixty, Errol looks a lot older. He is in love again and planning his fifth marriage after having twenty-five children with fifteen women. Errol taught himself journalism and mastered the craft while they were in prison.

He has lived by the saying "The pen is mightier than the sword" and wholeheartedly defends his right to publish.

Victor turns to look at the waitress as she sets out the scotch and water on the table. He follows Errol's beady eyes as they undress her.

"I thought you were planning to get married soon?" Victor asks.

"Just after the elections," Errol answers. "I will have a double celebration. The prime minister will be my best man."

Victor examines his friend. He looks constipated and his weight loss is noticeable. There are rumors that he is HIV positive. He lost his hair long ago and shaves off the remaining strands.

Errol wears scruffy, outdated clothes and a pair of cracked weather-beaten leather sandals. He is always fiddling and twitching and straightening up his glasses.

Errol is a deceptive workaholic who feels he has worked tirelessly without a break. He feels he has toiled without reward.

"Why are you watching the young lady this way?" Victor asks.

"Every day they're looking better."

"But you must control yourself."

"That's what I am doing." He tears his eyes away from the young girl to look at Victor. "I am only feasting my eyes."

Victor is glad to see his friend today. Despite the rumors, his outward presence is cheery.

He fears Errol's tendency to plan destruction and to dismantle organized opposition in favor of his own goals. Victor knows Errol is manic-depressive, unpredictably slipping into a debilitating depression and coming back out suddenly with renewed purpose. Still, he loves to be the one to get the job done.

"I met our boy, Richard, at the embassy."

"Our boy. He puts his resources behind Karl."

"Not anymore." Victor looks around. "They're pulling the plug on him this time."

"He told you so?"

"This is what he called me to his office to say."

"Then we win."

"Not so fast." Victor tempers his enthusiasm. "We still have to do our work."

The food arrives, and Victor eats at a steady pace. He catches Errol eyeing the waitress again.

"Tell me about your fiancée."

Errol rolls his eyes away from the waitress.

"She is gorgeous."

"How long have you known her?"

"Six months." Errol dabbles with the food. "She is a reporter. Started five months ago."

Victors watches him play with his food, only taking small bites as he sips the scotch. His friend's mental health worries him. Though he won't talk about it, Errol uses women to play out his sexual prowess and arousal fantasies.

Victor finishes eating and craves dessert. He signals the waitress.

"Not eating your food today, Mr. Bullen?" she asks.

"Wrap it," he tells her. "I will take it away. Seeing you, I lost my appetite for food." He slips a piece of paper into her hand.

Victor orders a mudslide and a cappuccino for dessert.

"You're eating for the both of us," Errol says.

"Dessert coming up, Prime Minister Calliste." The waitress smiles coyly as she clears the table.

"Not so fast," Victor says.

"Mr. Calliste, we win." She walks to the kitchen and disappears around the corner.

"What's the next move?" Errol asks.

"Write the story."

"Richard agreed to go public?"

"He will not tell me otherwise. He knows telling me is as good as telling you."

"I am on it."

"This election is ours."

***

Allyson is sitting in her car outside the school gate. Through the wave of children tumbling out of the schoolyard, she sees Clint and Cari holding hands as they approach the car. A smile brightens her face as she thinks of how fortunate they are.

She has no memory of her parents. She was told that her father never acknowledged her existence and her mother skated off to Canada, leaving her with her aging grandmother when Allyson was two.

As she grew, her interests varied. At primary school, she was a troublemaker who disrupted classes. In secondary school, she became a strong, celebrated athlete; her prowess earning her a sports scholarship to the University of Guyana.

University life was fun. She shopped and changed degree programs before settling on education. During that time, knowledge wasn't as important as fun and freedom.

Still, she welcomed the opportunity that education gave her—the chance to leave Guyana and start a new life on Mabuya Island.

"Mummy...Mummy," the children sing in unison as they climb into the car.

"Hi guys," she greets them and maneuvers the car into the traffic. "Tell me."

"Mummy, did Daddy go to prison?" Cari asks.

"Who told you that?"

"The other kids in our class. When we passed the prison on our trip today, they said Daddy was there."

"Cari, tonight while Daddy is putting you to bed, ask him. He will tell you."

"Was Daddy a murderer?"

"No dear, nothing so."

"Mummy, the children say the election's coming," Clint says.

"What did they say?"

"They say we will not be coming back to school."

"What do they mean?"

"They say Daddy will be the next prime minister, and he will send us to private school."

"Daddy will do no such thing. You guys have to stop listening to these children."

"But they are our friends, Mummy," Cari says.

"Anybody for pizza?"

"Yeah!" they chant.

"Let's have a president. What topping?"

"I want pineapple and pepperoni," Clint says.

"Ham and extra cheese for me," says Cari.

"One president pizza with extra toppings coming," Allyson announces as she pulls into the driveway of Mike's Café.

They enter the café and place their order. While they wait, Allyson looks at the children fooling around with each other and thinks of her luck, finally having a successful family.

She'd had many relationships and lost them, until Victor, an elder man, became a source of grounding for her, providing the parental guidance for their children that she never had as a child.

The pizza arrives, and she doles out the slices.

***

In the boardroom at the party headquarters, Victor looks at the men and the women gathered. He has confidence in them, believing they will excel in the upcoming contest. This is what he wants.

"It's in your hands," he addresses them. "This is our election to win. By all indicators, Karl is on the back foot and fading fast. General secretary, what are you hearing?"

"This is exactly the sentiment on the ground," Aadesh tells everyone. "In summary, Karl has exhausted his time among his party members and the people. He is willing to quit, but his ego won't let him. We are dealing with a desperate man approaching the twilight of his dictatorship. The situation worsens daily. He exhibits poor decision-making and loss of social and communication skills. His leadership style has failed him, so he encourages bullying."

Victor turns to the party chairman.

"What is your assessment?"

"In any contest, may the best man win. But the reading is consistent, this man is gone. I agree with our general secretary's assessment. For the first time in years, we are in the best position to win this election. This is what I have been picking up in my travels. People say the man is falling apart internally.

"In his Cabinet, he knows everything. He listens to no one and is stubborn and unyielding. At the end of the Cabinet, he doctors the minutes to suit his whims and fancies. The ministers sit there and do nothing. Members cannot debate or discuss ideas. He refuses to logically analyze any scenarios.

"I understand that he will not be using more than half of them in the upcoming elections. He plans to spit them out and bring in new people."

"What do you think?" Victor asks the party's chief financial officer.

"You mean apart from the stories about his many women?" she asks.

Victor and the others laugh.

"Let's hear it," Victor urges.

"His relationship with his wife is done. Michelle refuses be onstage with him in this campaign. She hangs on to the marriage because she does not believe in divorce. He is lucky she is the 'till death do us part' sort of woman. Can you guys explain his behavior? He thinks he is the greatest ram goat in the world?"

"We are not into that," one man replies.

The financial officer continues: "I know. I am only kidding. What is it? This man is shameless and bullheaded. Women are not safe around him. Once he gets his wish, he controls you. He has no love.

"He wants women who can do him favors. Friends with benefits. He loves to exercise his control over them. He will never tackle someone like me, for example. Karl avoids thinkers.

"Don't come between him and his money, though. He hoards money with no intention of losing it. Look out. In this election, he has a war chest to spend, but his weakness might be in holding back a large sum for himself."

Victor turns to the chairman of the party.

"Mr. Chairman? What are you hearing?"

"He is losing faith in himself and his people. Tasks are not delegated. He does everything himself. He cannot resolve problems. His decisions are incomplete and incorrect.

"He has no morality. With him, there are no gray areas; things are either black or white. His interpersonal relationships are dwindling due to demands placed on his friends and his women.

"Everyone knows him as a thief. He has lost respect. They see him as heartless and selfish. He is distrustful of others' motives and moves against his friends at the slightest utterance of a rumor showing disagreement with his Draconian policies.

"Victor, like you said, this man is on the back foot, so we must chase him from town."

Victor looks around at his colleagues, who are smiling. He feels calm. They are reliable. He values their analyses and respects their ability to come together to form a consensus and even to resolve conflicts. He loves their ability to work alone and unperturbed by stress. Each member can put aside his or her own needs to go along with the team. They hide their differences well.

Victor contributes a sense of reassurance, unity, and peace, yet he fears they will separate because of conflicts—they're great at hiding their contrary thoughts and ideas.

"This is a comprehensive analysis. I cannot add to it," he concludes. "We will meet again in two days. Meantime, intensify the groundwork."

"Gentlemen, I have a concern." Aadesh stops everyone with his grave voice. "I am concerned about the future leadership of our party. No disrespect to brother Victor, but the issue of leadership must be settled before I participate."

"Now is not the time," the chairman says.

"It's now or never," Aadesh states. "I need assurance."

"I will step down halfway through the term," Victor says.

"I can live with that," Aadesh states. "I want it in writing."

"I will not put it in writing," Victor affirms.

"What is your haste to become the leader?" the chairman asks.

"It is a matter of honoring a commitment," Aadesh says.

"I give you my commitment," Victor says. "That is the best I can do."

"We will see about that," Aadesh says.

"Comrades, I call this meeting to a close."

Victor remains seated while his party executive leaves. He watches Aadesh go. He knows he cannot not evade or postpone the leadership confrontation. It is also clear to him the party will not win the upcoming elections under Aadesh's leadership. Aadesh will not command the unity of the party or the population.

Unfortunately, Victor knows the man believes he is popular, loved, and born to lead. Aadesh has never been ordinary. Being the last of his father's ten sons, he was always the favorite. He was born at the time when the family owned several businesses and properties. He studied engineering at Massachusetts Institute of Technology, and returned to Mabuya to join any political organization that would have him.

Members of the party are aware of his contribution to the political campaign and the party's physical appearance. They are also aware of his lack of commitment to the party and his tendency to sell his wares to the highest bidder. It is no secret Aadesh is willing to buy what he wants, including the leadership of the party.

Aadesh thrives on the idea that he is loved by everyone, not necessarily members of a party. People follow him wherever he goes. He can move freely among the political parties without compunction or rebuke. Their love for him knows no bounds.

Victor is suspicious of Aadesh's calm reaction. He has seen the man's moodiness under pressure. Aadesh moves from laughing and grinning to somber and unresponsive in a flash, usually as he walks away from further discussion. Minutes later he can be relaxed, cheerful, and caring.

Aadesh has a woman and child in every parish. When he is not at work, he spends time with one of the women and the children. As a result, he has formed alliances with a broad base of individuals in rural and remote areas of the island. He has a wide audience who will support his leadership bid when he launches it.

The party will miss his unique creative skill and ability to attract people. They will not miss his moody, withdrawn character. Considering the balance of gains and losses, Victor believes the negative will outweigh the positive. During his withdrawn phases, Aadesh becomes inefficient and closed. He spends his time focusing on emotions instead of his tasks.

An extrovert by nature, his interaction with people is always shrouded in intrigue and mystery. At times he confuses his personal popularity with support for his political position. Victor believes the man is a child, refusing to grow. Constantly in search of an identity. Trying to fit into the society. Attempting to define himself. Using politics as an outlet for his suppressed energy. Setting the leadership as a goal to achieve. The ultimate definition of his life.

Victor knows he cannot allow the party to become a conduit of gratification for the ego of a lost child.

***

Victor looks over the stuffed brown envelope on his desk to lock eyes with Milosevic on the other side.

"I can give you more," Milosevic says. "I can finance your election campaign."

"This will defeat everything I stand for," Victor tells him.

"That was the old days," Milosevic says. "Nobody thinks that way anymore."

"Then I am prepared to be alone," Victor says. "It will not be the first time."

"You will not win this election without money." Milosevic says. "I will help you launch your candidates, run your advertising campaign, and pay the people you need to vote for you."

"We do not need you." Victor stands and walks to the water dispenser to fill a glass and continues to stand by the cannister. "Our campaign will be run on good governance, honesty, and integrity in public office. We intend to clean out central government, state bodies, and other public serving institutions of corrupt bureaucrats and incompetent management."

"How will you do this?" Milosevic asks.

"We plan to empower the public service commission and the other constitutional institutions set up to perform their specific roles. The public service commission will be able to hire and fire again. Political appointees will be purged from the ministries and sent to where they belong."

"People will not vote for you without money," Milosevic says, eyeing the envelope on the desk.

"Take your money and go, mister," Victor says. "The statutory bodies new mandate is to be profitable."

"Even if you come to office, you need to deal with investors like me," Milosevic says.

"My government will deal with investors," Victor says. "We will deal with them based on their own merit. I oppose foreign investors who believe they can pay bribes to politicians and other state officials to receive favors in the country. Come to the country with clean hands to invest your money in genuine developmental projects."

Milosevic retrieves the envelope from the desk and stands.

"You will not survive in politics." He sneers. "You are a dinosaur. The people who held your view are long gone. The modern world is run by people like Karl. They take what they get and distribute to the people. People no longer care who or where the money comes from, as long as they have it to spend."

"This is why we oppose Karl and his methods." Victor moves toward Milosevic, crowding him to the doorway. "We will never join the band of dishonest leaders whose only intention is to fill their pockets while in government. They claim they give all to the people, but I can tell you less than 1 percent of the amount you give to these men finds its way to the poor of this country."

"You will regret this," Milosevic says.

"Is that a threat?" Victor asks.

"No. It's a statement of fact," Milosevic says.

"My plans are to develop this country without the likes of you," Victor says. "In the past we have achieved 6 to 10 percent economic growth without you. Our economic strategy will use our own resources to promote growth."

"You are isolated and outdated." Milosevic raises his voice.

"Many countries refuse to tolerate people like you," Victor returns.

"They can't stop me," Milosevic says. "I am part of the modern business world."

"Singapore, Germany, Sweden, the UK, the European Union, and many others don't tolerate people like you," Victor says. "They have legislation aimed at stopping your practices and dealing with the people who encourage you."

Milosevic backs to the doorway as Victor advances.

My government will focus on implementation," Victor shouts. "There are enough ideas and projects on the records. We don't need more of you. We will roll up our sleeves and get it done. When we come to power, our people will develop a new sense of purpose, belonging, and drive to build this nation. I am clear in my vision of our place in the world as a member of the United Nations. They will look at us as a small nation daring to stand tall with bigger countries in stamping out corruption and fraud."

"You are a dreamer." Milosevic laughs.

"Yes, I am," Victor agrees. "I plan to lead in the old-fashioned way. By example. This country must return to exports. We used to compete with the world for quality. Our raw materials are blended with others to make quality products. Our unique exports are hard to copy and develop. Our cocoa is used to blend others to make pure chocolate for the connoisseurs. We grow spices here that cannot be found or duplicated elsewhere."

"With my project you don't need to export anything," Milosevic says.

"Leave us alone," Victor says. "We love our exports. We will free up production; increase job productivity; spend more on research, development, and innovation, while we invest in human capacity and shills. This island will be corruption free and development oriented. The nature of politics will change."

"After you lose the election, I will still have this money for you." Milosevic backs through the door clutching the envelope.

"You will never see that," Victor tells him.

***

Huddled over the hood of a 4x4 Double Cab pickup are four policemen examining a map. Swaggart is standing off to one side, drinking a beer. The sergeant is explaining to a corporal and two police constables several points on the map and marking them off.

"Fellas, the boss wants a smooth operation," Swaggart interjects. "In and out in a flash." He sips on his beer and snaps his fingers.

The sergeant turns from the map to watch Swaggart. For a moment, his eyes are fierce and uncompromising, then he softens slowly into a wry smile.

"Why you think he chose us?" the sergeant asks.

Swaggart takes another sip at his beer.

"I hear you guys get results," he answers. "The best."

"Then shut up. Watch and learn."

"I am cool." Swaggart shrugs. "Whoever you are. Just get it done."

The sergeant bends over the map again and points to a spot.

"The report says he will be here. We will hit him hard and fast. A quick in and out extraction."

"Sarge, do we need to notify anybody?" the corporal asks.

"No. This one is ours."

"Any backup?"

"No backup."

"Communications?"

"None."

"Strictly off the books?"

"Off the books, except that we will need to keep him overnight in the cell."

"Arms?"

"Semiautomatics and sidearms."

Swaggart guzzles the beer and walks closer to the men.

"Fellas, can I go now?" he asks.

"Get out of here. We don't need you."

Swaggart gets into a small SUV and drives away.

"Any other questions?" the sergeant asks his men.

"We good to go," the corporal answers.

"Let's roll."

The men enter the pickup and leave the area.

***

The pickup halts within a short distance of Ras's hut. Two police constables deploy and make their way to different sides of the hut. The vehicle quietly edges closer. The sergeant and the corporal get out and creep toward the rotten back door.

Ras is dressed in a Bob Marley T-shirt and drawers. He is leaning against a bamboo shelf, peeling a yam. A shuffling sound catches his attention. He stops to listen, and hearing nothing, he continues with his work.

He jumps when the sergeant shouts, "Ras, this is the police. Open the door."

At the same time, the makeshift door shatters to the ground as the sergeant bursts into the hut with his service pistol pointed at Ras.

Ras drops the knife and the yam and heaves out of the window. He lands on his feet outside only to be struck down by a gun butt from one of the police constables.

Falling to the ground, he holds the back of his head and turns to face his assailant.

"Wha me ah do?" Ras asks.

"Don't play dumb with us," says the constable.

"Well, arrest me," Ras says.

"We will."

"Ah en' do nuttin," Ras protests. "Ah en' going no-way."

"We will see," the constable barks. "Stand."

"Me nah do nuttin."

The policeman kicks Ras repeatedly in his rib cage.

"I told you to stand."

Ras is rolling on the ground weakly professing his innocence and try-ing to defend himself. The officers take turns beating him. One of the men returns to the pickup to retrieve a baton and bludgeons Ras with it.

"You wanna kill me?"

"You must learn to behave."

Two constables try to restrain Ras with full force. He uses his last strength to resist, standing and rushing toward them. They swat him to the ground.

In the end, the sergeant steps in and pepper-sprays Ras.

He twists as they drag him to the pickup and sling him into the bed. One of the constables handcuffs him to a ring in the bed of the vehicle. The other men jump in the cab, and they drive away.

CHAPTER SIX

Richard is bent over his desk. His piercing blue eyes drill into Karl. The tall, angular CIA agent looks at the small man before him.

"Hope you have a good reason for dragging me here," Karl snarls.

"What do you consider a good reason?" Richard asks.

"You tell me." Karl claims, "It's your call."

"Andre Milosevic."

"What about him?"

"Deport him," Richard demands.

"To where?"

"I don't care." Richard is livid. "Wherever will take him. Better still, let the bastard choose."

"Why?"

"He is a crook and a security risk. Is that enough reason for you?"

"Straight away?"

"You have twenty-four hours."

"I need more time."

Richard straightens up, making Karl look even smaller. "You do not have more time."

"You brought me here for this?"

"That should tell you the importance."

"Fine. Fine. Lighten up, man. We are friends."

Karl rises to leave. Richard steps around the desk and walks him to the door.

"Remember, you have twenty-four hours or we escalate."

"What do you mean?"

"You've known me long enough. I do not bluff. We will just escalate."

Karl pauses at the door. "Richard, who is behind this?"

"Don't play innocent with me." Richard matches Karl's eyes. "You know how this works. The decision is yours, whether he goes alone or with you."

Karl's perplexity is unmistakable as he storms out of the building.

***

Jules is sitting on a locally made barstool in the kitchen, while his mother is on a chair facing him. The housekeeper is preparing brunch. She serves corned fish in grated carrots, seasoning peppers, coo-coo, bush yam, and herbal tea.

"Jules, I know you will love this," the housekeeper says, placing a refrigerated jar on the table.

"Coconut water," he says without tasting it.

"You know the thing," she says.

"They say it's not good for my condition," his mom says.

"It's better to be safe," Jules says.

Jules dives into the spread before him and devours his food.

"I have more," the housekeeper says.

"Bring it." Jules rubs his stomach.

She refills his plate. Jules attacks the food and glances at his mother's untouched plate.

"Mom, you're not eating?" he asks.

"Maybe later," she says, continuing to watch him eat.

The housekeeper signals to Jules from behind his mother's back. Her mouth forms a silent *no*.

"Are you losing your appetite?" he asks.

"I am fine. How are you doing?" she asks.

"I am doing good. We are preparing for elections."

"Are you running again?" she asks.

"Karl says he will make the changes and let us know," he says.

"*Karl says*. Do you plan to die working for this dictator?" she asks, pursing her mouth.

"Mom, not now," he says. He looks to the housekeeper. The woman turns toward the sink to wash the dishes.

"When?" she asks.

"Another time," he answers.

"Tomorrow is not yours," she says.

"I will wait to see if he picks me to run for the seat again."

"Why do you have to? You were not this guy. I know you as a child with drive and initiative. You wanted to be your own boss. When will that happen?" his mother queries.

"Mom, I am working on it."

"Stop working and do," she says.

"Why are you so upset?" he asks.

"First of all, time doesn't belong to you. You are waiting on a dead man's boots. Second, you are sharper than, brighter than, and superior to that half-wit you work for. You are the one who is making him look good. Third, a father is a sperm donor, but integrity comes from your mother's womb. The evil of a mother passes to her children."

"Trust me, Mom. I have it under control."

"It's your life."

"Coconut ice cream, Jules?" the housekeeper interrupts.

"My favorite." Jules is glad for the distraction.

***

Back at his office, Karl is meeting with Cathy Gordon. Her gray eyes always unnerve him, her deadpan features reminding him of Maya Angelou.

He surveys her short hair, powerful arms and legs and wonders what her body looks like under her executive dress suit.

"Somebody is leaking secrets from my Cabinet."

"Who?"

Anger flashes across his face, and he resists the temptation to use obscene language. Is this woman doubting his credibility? Challenging him?

Karl doesn't know her well. They told him she was educated, fifty, married, and had dedicated her life to public service. He heard she was good at rallying the leadership of the organization and getting everyone to play their role in the interest of development.

He had guessed she might be trouble—her esoteric interests being more important than total devotion to his government.

"Are you doubting me?" he asks.

"No, prime minister."

"Your facial expression speaks for itself."

"Excuse me, sir?"

"They tell me you are rude."

"I am sorry."

"You are not sorry. Look at you, sitting there trying to impress me. You are one of those who believes you are better than my ordinary people. You pretend to be high and mighty. Little Miss Perfect. People like you hate my grassroots approach. You hold yourself as if I am low class and you are better. You are right and I am wrong. I stand for evil, while you are good.

"Look at you. Stiff and sarcastic. I am sure you love your dog more than human beings."

"I don't know what to say." Cathy settles in the chair.

"I didn't ask you to say anything. I made up my mind. You must be moved out of the Cabinet office."

"It is your prerogative, prime minister."

"I know."

"I urge you to follow the procedures of the Mabuya Public Service Commission."

Karl feels his anger rise. She is giving him advice like she is the one in charge.

"This meeting is over."

***

Errol is on the phone at the office of the *Mabuya Voice* newspaper. Through the glass partition, he can see reporters hacking away at their computers or milling around collecting drafts from the printer. Errol is listening intently to Richard.

"I have a hot one for you," Richard tells him. "I have your boy on tape accepting a bribe from Andre Milosevic. If you don't hear from me within twenty-four hours, run the story. I will not give you the tapes now. They are my aces in the hole."

"Should I quote you?" Errol asks.

"Don't be foolish."

"Just checking. I wanted to tighten the noose."

"We are not ready to throw him under the bus yet. Just shake him up."

"I am on it."

"Good."

***

Karl tells Colonel Lester Bynoe, "We need to hand over Milosevic, but he cannot know we were involved."

"Leave it to me," Colonel Bynoe says.

"All right, I will leave that in your hands. How is the political situation on the island?"

"As you know, there is talk that you received huge sums of money as bribes to favor Milosevic and implement his projects. The leader of the opposition is willing to give evidence that he was approached by Milosevic with bribe money to finance his election campaign. This has been leaked and will certainly be printed in the papers this week. The nation and the region are on fire with this one."

Karl looks fiercely at the colonel. "Don't they understand that it's my money?"

"I think they do," the colonel answers, "but they hate Milosevic."

"Well, he is good as gone now."

"Okay. You made the decision to call an early election."

"I cannot change that now." Karl glares at the colonel.

"I will need more information to prepare," the colonel answers.

"Certainly, certainly. You will get the information," Karl says.

"Sir, you are aware that you will need to make changes to your team."

"Naturally. Most of them have not even uttered a single word in my defense."

The colonel rises from his seat.

"Is this all, sir?" he asks.

"For now. Keep me updated on Milosevic," Karl demands.

"I will. You have a good day, PM."

The colonel leaves the office.

Karl pulls a cell phone from his pocket and walks toward the window. He punches a few numbers in and puts the phone to his ear.

***

In his office, Richard hangs up the phone, walks over to the television, and plays the video with Karl and Milosevic in the hotel room. He watches the clip up to the point where Karl leaves the room, then he switches off the television.

"Fool." Embarrassed and exhausted, he slumps into his chair.

The light touch around his neck jolts him. He forgot Diana was there.

She pulls her hand away.

"Jumpy?" she asks.

"Don't stop," he says.

She massages his neck.

"This is the Milosevic guy?"

"Yeah."

"Karl went personally to collect."

"He trusts no one."

"But he uses Jules most of the time."

"This one was too big for Jules," Richard says. "The greedy man had to go for himself."

"He has used me as well," Diana reveals.

"You never told me that."

"Many times."

"How?"

"A stranger will meet me and say, 'Hold this for the man.'" Diana demonstrates colleting a package with her hands.

"What do you do with the money?" Richard asks.

"I stash it away in an account that he has access to."

"He has never asked for it?"

"No. From time to time he tells me the balance," Diana says.

"I don't want to know," Richard says. "If I know more, I will have to commence proceeding for forfeiture."

"I should have told you before," Diana says.

"What do you think he is relying on to win this election?" Richard asks. "I get the feeling that he has a trump card up his sleeve. There is something he is not telling everybody."

"His mother."

"That dainty old lady."

"She holds the key to his success," Diana says.

"His mother? You've lost me," Richard says. "Thank you for reminding me I wasn't born on this island. So many cultural matters I don't understand."

"The obeah they work is for real," Diana says. "One minute, Karl is a genuine, kindhearted, well-mannered, and reasonable man. Within moments you will swear you're dealing with a different man, a man possessed, demonic, controlled by an external power, arrogant, and self-opinionated.

"Are you seriously suggesting that he will stake his political career on his mother's obeah?" Richard asks.

"Richard, everything this man does is guided by his belief in black arts and the practice of witchcraft. I will bet you that his selection of the date for the election was influenced by this belief."

"Diana, this is enough." Richard raises his hands in surrender.

"Fine," Diana says.

CHAPTER SEVEN

The white Toyota Corolla pulls into Rita Stone's yard, and Karl opens the door and gets out. His mother is sitting on the verandah with Kenny. Karl storms past them and goes into the house. They follow him.

"Karl, what's the matter now?" Rita asks. "Who upset you?"

Karl sits at the dining table, his mouth set and his eyes fiery.

"If you don't tell us, we can't help you," Kenny begs. "We are family. Since Dad died, we are all you've got."

"They are after me," Karl hisses. "They want to destroy me."

"They will not succeed, son." Rita is firm. "Not while I am around." She heads to the kitchen. Kenny pulls up a chair across from Karl.

"What is the issue?" Kenny asks.

"Richard is behind it," he admits. "He has a tape with Andre giving me money."

"Jesus, why didn't you send somebody?"

"Who?" Karl is livid. "So they could steal it?"

"I could have gone," Kenny suggests.

"They would still blame me."

"Tell the people Andre owed you money and you went to collect it."

"What could Andre owe me for?"

"I dunno. Maybe he sponsored your last trip?"

"Makes sense. Go on."

"He sponsored your last trip, and he was reimbursing you."

"Yeah."

"That's it."

Rita returns to the dining section carrying two cups of tea.

"You boys are looking better." She smiles. "Karl, when they interfere with you, come to me."

She places a cup of steaming brew in front of each son and walks away.

"I am going to read a psalm on their heads now," she says.

Karl takes a sip and cringes.

"Kenny, have you ever found out what she puts in this thing?"

"Nah." Kenny shrugs. "That's her closely guarded secret, but I know a few of the ingredients."

Karl smiles for the first time. He puts his hand on Kenny's shoulder.

"I think we have cracked it," he says.

"Cheers, let's put this tea on the market." The brothers toast.

"You're welcome, bro."

They burst into laughter simultaneously.

***

Errol is pacing the floor. "Start drafting the story," he tells his subeditor. "Front page. If necessary, we will dump it. For now, gather information on Andre Milosevic, his woman, his associates, and his relationship with Karl. I will fill in the rest."

"Is Andre on the island?" the subeditor asks.

"Yeah," Errol answers. "Find out where he is staying. See if you can get pictures."

The subeditor hops around the office.

"You think we have him this time?"

"You never know," Errol says. "That slippery bastard. He might pull another stunt. Get on it."

The subeditor speeds out of the office.

***

Karl is leaning over the verandah of his official residence. His security guard takes a call as a Range Rover stops at the security booth at the foot of the hill. He whispers into Karl's ear as if there are people around listening.

"Let him come," Karl says. "I want to know what brings him here."

The gate opens and the vehicle drives up the hill to the great house, which stands at the top of a concrete road surrounded by mahogany trees and a variety of flowers.

The colonial house was constructed in phases with later renovations to the original structure. The exterior walls were sand plastered and painted cream. The roof is now pre-painted corrugated metal. A large porch stretches and wraps halfway around one side. Extensions were made to accommodate maids' living quarters and sleeping rooms for the security detail. Other concrete buildings at the back serve as garages and storage facilities. The walls are reinforced to repel small-arms fire and other light mortar attacks.

The British architecture was adapted to the tropics with jalousies and sash windows along the verandah, allowing cool breezes to sweep through. The front doors open into a spacious hall with a staircase in the center.

Karl looks on as the vehicle parks in the yard and Aadesh Hamid exits. The man walks up the stairs, holding on to the iron balustrades to join Karl on the verandah.

"Have a seat," Karl says. "Can I offer you a drink?"

"Coffee," Aadesh requests.

Karl commands the maid to bring the coffee and a fruit shake for himself.

"Talk to me." Karl does not hesitate.

"I come with a proposal," Aadesh announces.

"Let's have it," Karl says.

"I want to join your party," Aadesh proposes.

"What's wrong with yours?" Karl asks, giggling.

"Too much bickering and infighting," Aadesh confesses.

"I thought you all were going to win the election," Karl states.

"No way," Aadesh says.

"You're tired of Victor." Karl feels like he has won a battle.

"Yes," Aadesh confirms.

"Welcome." Karl reaches out and taps the man on his shoulder.

"Victor is obsessed with winning the election. He does not show it on the outside, but he wants to be in power badly. He thinks he is the only man to bring salvation to this land. This is what I fear. The conceit that he is a deliverer." Aadesh raises his voice.

"When are you suggesting?" Karl asks.

The maid returns with the drinks.

"I can cross sides as soon as you ready," Aadesh states.

"Today," Karl says.

"Okay." Aadesh is eager.

"You can run for the city," Karl suggests.

"That's all I need," Aadesh responds.

"We agree, then," Karl says.

"Of course. This will piss off Victor. He cannot handle losing people around him. Under pressure, he buckles. When he is relaxed and in control, he is a different man," Aadesh says.

"I know Victor well," says Karl. "When we were in the same party, he always complained that people felt they were better than him. People had more education than him. Most of his knowledge was picked up along the way. This made him feel inferior. He gives people this calm, in-control impression so they think they can rely on him.

"He knows how to bring people together to resolve conflicts, but he withdraws himself from the negative consequences of decisions he makes. This man pretends to be a peacemaker and to love teamwork, but he always does his own thing. Under the smooth exterior is a volcano waiting to erupt," Karl says.

"You know him well," Aadesh mumbles.

"The worst comes when you break away from him. Don't expect him to talk to you again," Karl states.

"I have moved on," Aadesh confirms.

"It's for the best," Karl says.

Karl stands to see Aadesh leave.

Later, Karl is sitting by the bar in his living room sipping a glass of red wine when Jules enters carrying a brown paper bag.

"I didn't want to hold your business overnight," Jules says.

He hands Karl the bag.

"From whom?"

"The Canadians," Jules says. "Thanks for the contract award."

Karl puts the bag on the bar and sits.

"Have a drink, Jules. What do you want?"

Jules sits. "Scotch on the rocks."

Karl puts ice into a glass and pushes away the ice bucket. He pours the scotch and hands the drink to Jules.

"You will be among the first to know this, but the opposition is coming after me with a new attack. They will say I am on tape accepting money from Andre Milosevic.

"What is our plan?"

"To go out there and tell people that this is just another attack from the haters."

"How do you explain the money?"

"Andre owed me money and was paying me back."

"Let's hit the road with it."

"Good. I will let you know when to strike."

Jules finishes his scotch and gets up to leave.

"Have a good night then."

"Great."

Karl sees Jules to the door.

***

Clint is hanging on to Victor's leg as he knocks at Cari's bedroom door for a second time.

He hears a shuffling inside the room but no response. Allyson joins them.

"Cari, please open the door," he begs. "Cari, please?"

"Go away," she shouts.

Allyson knocks.

"Cari, darling, can I come in?" she asks.

"Yes, you can, Mummy," Cari answers. "Not him."

The door pops open, and Cari runs to her bed and dives under the sheet.

Allyson and Clint enter, leaving the door ajar.

"Cari, please listen to Daddy." Allyson sits at the side of the bed and gently pulls the sheet from over Cari's head. "Let him come in, and he will tell you everything. Then he will read a lovely story to you. I know you will love it."

Cari bites her lip, thinking it over. She tugs at the sheet and covers her head. They continue to beg. Finally, she pulls down the sheet and shakes her head in agreement. Allyson signals for Victor to enter.

Victor sits on the other side of the bed.

"I did nothing wrong, Cari. Let me explain," Victor says. "Will you give Daddy a chance?"

She shakes her head.

"In life you will meet good people and bad people," Victor says. "Do you understand?"

She signals agreement.

"Good people will treat you with respect and help you along the way. Bad people will harm you. They will cheat you."

Cari sits up in her bed.

"These bad people didn't want me. In their own interest, they thought it was best to lock me up for my beliefs, for my values."

"Why didn't you tell us before, Daddy?" Clint asks.

"I wanted you to be older. When you could understand."

"Listen, guys, your dad was only trying to be protective."

"Did you kill people, Daddy?"

"No," Victor says. "It was nothing bad."

"Okay, Dad." Cari removes more of the cover and extends her arms for a hug. Victor welcomes her with a warm embrace and rubs her back.

"Let me tell you the story about the wolf in sheep's clothing. Some people will come to you pretending to be something else. Do not allow them to fool you. This shepherd was strong and vigilant. He guarded his sheep with his life, so though the wolf wanted to eat the sheep, he couldn't come close.

"One day the wolf found a discarded sheepskin. He put it on and strolled among the sheep. He succeeded in getting a few sheep to follow him. He drew them off to one side and ate them. This went on for a while until the shepherd realized his number of sheep was dropping; he realized something was wrong.

"He searched among his sheep until he found the wolf and killed him."

Victor looks at Cari sleeping. Clint is lying across the bed, and Allyson smiles at the end of the story. He tucks in Cari and carries Clint to his room.

***

Karl pulls on a T-shirt and sits on the bed. Michelle is leaning against the headboard reading the Lord's Prayer.

"You not going anywhere tonight, Karl?" she asks.

"No."

"Your appetite cut."

"What you mean?"

"The news shrink your cock?"

"What do you mean?"

"Don't be coy with me."

"Well, explain."

"Let me repeat in case you hard of hearing. The news you got today shrink your cock and clamp your ball? Do you hear me now?"

"Yes, but what news?"

"Karl, you can play this game with other people but not with me. Never forget that I am the one who introduced you to Richard."

Karl bolts under the covers, turns his back to Michelle, knowing it will be hell for him to fall asleep. Michelle grins, then continues reading her prayer book.

CHAPTER EIGHT

Victor sits by the makeshift bar on the beach as Allyson and the children run off to the extreme end. He watches them disappear into the dense shrubbery in search of adventure. They will climb the rocky incline to the clearing at the top. A short walk will take them to an old Amerindian cave to hunt for treasure and play hide-and-seek.

"They will be fine," Errol says, pulling up a stool to join him.

"I know," Victor says. "They know how to safeguard themselves."

"I should have brought my wife and children," Errol says.

"It's a family fun day; everyone is welcome," Victor says.

He looks across to the other side of the beach where the party members and supporters are spread out playing games and discussing in groups.

"Great turnout," Errol says.

"If we had free transportation, there would be more," Victor states. "Some people don't have the money to pay the transportation cost to come here."

"It is hard to get to," Errol says. "White Horse Bay, one of the island's best-kept secrets."

"One of many. All waiting to be explored," Victor declares.

He turns to look at the calm, pristine water, protected by the barrier reef one hundred meters away and shielded by the protruding rocks on both sides. The sand is not the most beautiful, powder-white type found on more popular beaches but a creamy color with touches of gray, hinting at its volcanic past.

"Do you know why they call it White Horse Bay?" Errol asks.

"My father told us the story," Victor says. "The legend of the White Horse. The plantation owner and his friends used this area for smuggling. There is a channel through the reef that allows small craft to come into the bay. One had to be careful since the tide can turn and bang your craft into the reef. The owner would dress his horse in white and ride it backward along the bay, especially on moonlit nights. People were scared to come to the beach even during the day. Long after he was dead and buried, people said they saw him riding the horse on the beach."

"Was there something about a coffin?" Errol asks.

"They would store the smuggled goods in coffins and lay them out along the beach for pick-up," Victor explains.

"People from the village saw these things?" Errol asks.

"To add to the eerie feeling, the men used to light up the beach with flambeau, creating weird shadows along the sand, into the water, and across the vegetation," Victor says.

"There was talk about selling souls," Errol suggests.

"According to my father, from time to time, the odd man would ignore the stories and brave the water; he'd get bashed along the reef line and die. Whenever that happened, they would say it was the work of the devil and the owner selling innocent souls," Victor answers.

"Today it's ours," Errol says.

"Thanks to the fight of our fathers against backwardness and ignorance," Victor states.

Victor scans the increasing crowd as the DJ increases the volume of the music. People dance and sway to Jimmy Cliff's version of "Many Rivers to Cross." He'd instructed them to play conscious lyrics for the duration of the activity, no slack and obscene music.

"What is the significance of today's activity to you?" Errol asks.

"It is unique. We, as a party, focus on the family. The family as a unit will propel the village, the village will propel the parish, and the parish will propel the country," Victor says.

"I suppose this occasion is even more important than others?" Errol asks.

"We come here every year. Sometimes more than once per year," Victor says. "We do other activities as well, but this event is critical given the election. This is how we will survive in or out of office."

"Are you happy with the response?"

"I feel great. People are still pouring in."

"I notice you are censoring the music."

"Only conscious lyrics. We want songs to motivate our people. Stimulate the minds of the children and focus on building a responsible society."

"Can that cost you votes?"

"A price I am willing to pay."

"What if people see you as uncompromising?"

"In some respects, I am. There are issues for the negotiating table. There are matters for discussion and agreement after compromise. Our fundamental principles are not of those."

"Even the food seems censored."

"Local food mainly. Ground provisions, fish, local chicken on the grill, freshly squeezed juices, and local spring water. We didn't ban other foods, but this is what we encourage. I mean we also have macaroni pie, rice and peas, and potato fries."

"You seem to enjoy this environment?" Errol probes.

"I get to relax. I blend in with the people, and we bond."

"What do you say to the people who don't know this side of you and call you stiff?"

"They don't know." Victor is adamant. "They label me. These labels stick without a hint of truth."

"What do you think attracts people most to this day?"

"It is uplifting, spiritual, and relaxing. The atmosphere is positive. The air is charged with positive energy. The activity includes and appeals to everyone. The young, the old, and in between. You leave here fueled, energized, and ready for action. It's like the power of the Holy Ghost."

"Are you looking forward to winning?"

"Errol, it's a contest. May the best man win. We have put forward our policies. People know what we stand for. They understand our position. I would love to win. If I lose, so be it. Life continues."

"What do you and Karl have in common?"

"Nothing."

"Has it always been like that?"

"There was a time when we fought for the same principles. We had similar ideals and goals. They say power corrupts, and the more absolute the power, the more corrupting. We have drifted apart over the years. He used to have a family; he doesn't anymore. He believed in justice and fair play; that is gone. The man has turned into a brutal dictator. Listens to no one. Rules his colleagues with an iron fist. We are miles apart."

"What will guarantee that you do not become this way once you taste the power?"

"Term limits. I believe in two terms. There is life after office. I admire the men who have served their country and can now relax and enjoy the remainder of their days. I have faith in the youth of this country. They will carry on. Put another way, they will have to carry on since none of us will be around forever."

"I have had a full interview with the future prime minister. Unplanned." Errol laughs.

"I promise you the first interview when my party comes into office."

"Let's drink to that."

***

Cathy is in her new office at the Ministry for Human Resource Development, where Karl had her transferred for challenging his authority. Cathy's secretary pokes her head around the slightly open door.

"Minister Bourne is here to see you."

"Tell him come in," Cathy tells her.

Minister Jules Bourne boldly slides past the secretary and enters the office.

"Good morning," he greets her.

Cathy invites him to have a seat and asks, "What brings you to my abode?"

"This could be a social visit."

"I know it's not."

"You caught me."

She surveys Jules. She could never understand his determination to protect Karl, seeing that he appeared always in control. With Jules's sense of purpose, how could he allow himself to be dispatched to do Karl's dirty work?

"Sock it to me. I am a big girl." Kathy thumps her chest with her fist.

"I can see that." He laughs.

"So, tell me."

"Don't take this the wrong way, but I suggest you take holidays."

"Why."

"It's in your best interest."

"I don't understand."

"This is a window of opportunity I am trying to open for you."

"And I'm supposed to jump out this window and break my neck on the other side?"

"It is safe and benefits both sides," the minister claims. "Take the route that's being offered."

She'd heard Jules was relentless in his need to please his master. She knows failure is not a choice for him since Karl uses him to ramrod his way to success. She can tell Jules is ready to bulldoze his way through her to win Karl's favor. Neither cares about the plight of others.

Control. This quality kept them together. They do not expect people to stand up to them.

"Sorry, I do not need holidays."

"Then they will send you on paid leave"

"You're working at the Public Service Commission now."

"I am a minister."

"That I know."

"I can offer you a scholarship to study in London."

"No, thank you. I have a husband and child at home."

"They can go with you."

"No. They don't want people dictating their lives."

"I take it you refuse the window."

Cathy is determined not to be a part of Karl's collection of robotic 'yes people' who do not question their actions or stand up for their rights.

"You can close it."

Jules pulls out two letters from his pocket and hands them to her.

"These are for you."

He marches out of the office without saying goodbye.

The first letter is from the governor general transferring her to a post not yet determined by the Public Service Commission. The second is also from the PSC, appointing her to the post that does not exist.

Cathy packs away her belongings.

***

Allyson is at a shop in the mall. She is enjoying the soft caress of a floral print dress on her skin when she hears Diana's voice. She turns to greet her friend.

"How you doing, girl?" Diana asks.

"I'm great," Allyson says.

"Planning to buy this one?"

"Not sure." Allyson pulls the dress off the rack and places it against her body. "How does it look?"

"It's lovely, girl. Have it."

"I think I will."

They walk to the cash point, and Allyson pays for the dress.

"What are your plans?" Diana asks.

"Got my dress. I'm done here," says Allyson.

"Let's have a drink and chat."

"Sure, I have time before I pick up the kids."

The two women walk to the food court and select a table near a window.

"I am having a mixed fruit smoothie," Diana says. "What do you want?"

"I will have the same."

Allyson watches Diana walk to the bar. Although they are on different sides of the political spectrum, they have remained friends through the years. Their friendship has always been challenged by Allyson's impulsive nature. Her ambitiousness is what first attracted Diana, but that wears thin easily. Allyson will dump a friend in a second if she feels that friend is affecting her negatively.

Diana returns with the smoothies, and they sip on the drinks.

"Lovely," purrs Allyson.

"The best," Diana choruses.

"What brings you to the mall today, girl? Not enough work at the ministry?" Allyson is curious.

"Nothing is happening, only election talk."

"Yeah. Your boy Karl is on a roll."

"My boy?" Diana frowns.

"You know what I mean," Allyson says coyly.

"No. I don't. What are you implying?"

"Nothing."

"You think I am one of those women who sleeps with him for power?" Diana demands.

"Darling, I never said that."

"You must have heard the rumors," she tells Allyson.

"I don't pay attention to them."

"Do you think I am with him?" Diana asks Allyson accusingly.

"I don't think."

Allyson wants her friend to control her feelings. This is the point where she gets the urge to walk away from people. Allyson thinks she knows what will help Diana find happiness—she just needs to release tension and go with the flow. She believes relaxing will allow Diana to live life on its own terms, peacefully.

"What is the accusation? You don't get involved in gossip," Diana tells Allyson.

"Thank you very much, I don't," Allyson responds confidently.

"Who do you think will win the elections?"

"You tell me."

"I might not be involved in either side," Diana announces.

"Why?"

"The man says he wants new blood. Fresh meat."

"He will lose. He will go bonkers."

"Victor has work for me?" Diana asks Allyson.

"Yes."

"Tell Victor I am serious. Leave a job for me. I am not sinking with Karl."

"I will tell him."

"Girl, you are a friend to have." Diana holds Allyson's hand tightly. "You want another drink?"

Allyson looks at her empty glass.

"Nah, I'd better get going."

The women stand and hug each other.

"Don't forget me," Diana whispers into Allyson's ear.

***

The tapping sound on her window next to the front door jolts Cathy from her midmorning doze. It has become a pattern over the past few weeks, since she's been home from work—laze in the living room, read a book, and doze off until midday. She rolls off the couch and stands, pulling her robe around her body.

"Who is it?" she asks.

"Colonel Bynoe," he says.

"Give me a few minutes to get dressed!" she shouts.

"Take your time," he says.

She hurries to the bedroom, dropping her robe on the way. What could the colonel want? Did Karl send him? She doubts that. He's always been pleasant to her. Saying, things like, "I've got your back. You are doing a good job; keep functioning."

In the bathroom, she brushes her teeth, splashes water on her face. She drags on a pair of sweatpants and an old polo, then returns to the living room.

In the living room, she looks at the dump and shudders. Rubbish is everywhere. The place has not been cleaned for weeks. This is no time for visitors. She opens the front door.

"Come in, Colonel," she says. "Excuse the state of the place. I didn't plan on entertaining visitors."

"That's okay, dear," Bynoe says. "I will sit over here." He picks a clean stool by the bar.

"Welcome to my humble abode," she says.

"Thank you."

"What brings a man of your caliber into these woods?"

"I was passing. My usual rounds. I decided to check on you."

"With all due respect, Colonel, you sure you're not on duty?"

"Never."

"Just making sure."

"I heard you were home, and I made a mental note to check on you any time I passed this way again," the colonel says.

"That is good of you," she says, walking toward the kitchen. "I am making a cup of tea. Do you want one?"

"Lovely," he says.

Cathy flicks on her kettle and selects two cups from the cupboard, washes them, and searches for the tea bags. She knows it is unfair, but the resentment is boiling inside her. From her knowledge of the operations of his government, she understands Karl's fierce protection of his turf. But this does not help to understand the people around him. They sit there and soak in the blows. No one speak out, no descents.

For the past few weeks, she had felt under pressure, angry, unappreciated, and alone. No one to turn to and no one reaching out to her. She'd contemplated breaking all rules, starting a new life, and becoming more comfortable with herself. Disposing of the urge to serve her country and to please her government.

She remembers the colonel passing in the shop by her mother. Sometimes he came alone, other times with a group of friends. They would play dominoes and eat and drink past midnight and into the early hours of the morning. Her father would spend a short while with them but went to bed early. During that time, the colonel and her mother developed a bond of mutual friendship and respect.

She knows that Colonel Bynoe isn't visiting her by accident. Accidents were not a part of his arsenal.

"What's on your mind, Colonel?"

"I am the one who recommended you as Cabinet secretary," he says. "Somehow I feel responsible for you."

"You shouldn't," she tells him. "I can handle my battle."

"By staying home and feeling sorry for yourself?" he asks. He surveys the unkempt kitchen and living room area. Her eyes follow his.

"This is only recent," she says, placing the cup of tea on the bar counter. He sips on it, continuing his surveillance. Eventually he zeroes his stare in on her. His eyes move as he analyzes.

She feels he can see beneath her persona. The calm, collected, and dependable worker at the highest level in the government service is really a lost unstable soul crying for help in silence. In the absence of her mother and father, she has no confidante. In addition, her alignment with rules at work and her insistence on laws and regulation hides an unprotected, anxious, and indecisive individual.

Cathy is aware that she has a problem dealing with people. She has lost many friends along the way and several more since being home.

"I have a suggestion." The colonel sips the tea, stands, and walks to the window. "You need to fight this guy."

"Alone?"

"Why not?"

"I cannot do this on my own."

"You are not alone." The colonel turns away from the window and returns to the bar. He selects a pen from the many strewn around the counter, grabs a piece of paper, and scribbles a name and a number. "This is your man. Tell him I spoke to you. He will take care of you."

"Colonel?" She looks into his eye for the first time. "Aren't you risking your job?"

"When we lose the election, I will have no job," he says.

"What can I expect to happen?" she asks.

"Discuss your matter with him. He will guide you going forward."

Cathy drags her eyes away from Colonel Bynoe. She wonders about his motivation.

"Why are you helping me?" she asks.

"You need it," he says. "You were genuine in your efforts to build and reform the public service. I thought you were honest and focused in your approach. The standards you set for yourself and workers will continue to improve the operations of the public service long after you leave. The staff are aware that your efforts were sincere. Others felt offended. People were jealous of your position. You might have stepped on their toes without knowing. They rejected your vision. This includes the top man."

"Thank you." She feels a sense of relief. "I will call to discuss my matter."

"That will be great," Colonel Bynoe says. "Thank you for the tea. I suggest you get out of your slumber and strengthen your resolve for the fight ahead."

"I will follow your advice," she says firmly.

***

The lone black SUV snakes its way through the Mabuya countryside and climbs out of the valley into the lush vegetation on the mountainside. Two thousand feet above sea level, Kenny is at the wheel squinting at the misty road ahead. Karl and Rita are in the back seat. They drive past the lake and begin their descent into the valley on the other side of the island.

Rita squeezes Karl's hand as Kenny maneuvers through the narrow road and stops outside a church. Karl and Rita exit the car, while Kenny hides the vehicle around the back of the building.

Karl and Rita hurry toward the entrance and enter the chapel. Kenny catches up with them, and they walk down the aisle and through an inconspicuous door leading to an inner sanctum.

Pastor Providence is kneeling before a small altar with his back toward them. He is concocting a mixture on the ground in front of him. He works energetically, and at one point, he tastes the mixture for potency.

The pastor is wearing full ceremonial dress—a long, flowing black robe with red stripes held together by a gold waistband. His assistant wears a gold turban wrapped with straps falling on either side of his head. He has on soft bedroom slippers.

The elevated altar is draped with rainbow-colored cloths. Lights flicker from a hundred colored candles, casting eerie shadows around the room. Paintings, carvings, and insignia adorn the walls.

"Your mother tells me they are trying to get rid of you," Pastor Providence says. He does not face them.

Karl starts to answer, but Rita silences him.

The pastor gets up from his kneeling position and glides around the room. A loud crackle shakes the room. He seems to float around his domain to land in front of Karl. His long gown flaps through the air. He's an albatross with beady eyes masked by the war paint on his face with a darker, blackened emphasis around the eyes and mouth.

Karl faints and falls into the arms of Rita and Kenny. They lay him on his back on a nearby mattress with the pastor waiting to attend to him.

Pastor wastes no time. He straddles Karl, forces his jaws open, and pours a full glass of the mixture he was preparing into Karl's throat. Karl, now conscious, perspires and convulses severely, retching on the floor of the sanctuary.

Something flutters in the vomit. It looks like a lizard with the ears of a bat and the wings of a newly hatched bird, and it starts growing by the second. Kenny and Rita hold on to Karl.

The pastor covers the creature with a metal urn from nearby. He pours mentholated spirits through the holes in the urn, pulls a candle, and lights the little thing. A blood-curdling sound echoes throughout the church as the beast beats around and dances to its death by fire in the urn.

Karl passes out again. Kenny, Rita, and Pastor Providence form a ring around him and mumble inaudible phrases. The pastor pulls a small vial of smelling salts from his gown and passes it under Karl's nose. He returns to consciousness.

They carry him out through the back door of the building and place him on the rear seat of the vehicle. He lies across the entire seat, then curls up in a fetal position. Kenny climbs into the driver's seat, while Rita sits in the front passenger seat. They wave goodbye to the pastor and settle in for the long journey home.

CHAPTER NINE

Errol Bullen is at his desk in the office as his cell phone rings. He answers. Karl is on the line.

"Just shut up and listen," Karl commands. "For the upcoming elections, I will clean out the old guard. Jules Bourne and Diana James will not be running this election. I am not satisfied that they defended me during this crisis and the others. Seventy-five percent of my candidates will be new blood."

Karl ends the call, and Errol places the phone on the table.

*****

Jules is at Victor's office. He hates these assignments, but loyalty doesn't allow him to refuse them. He looks at the artist impression of the new Mabuya General Hospital hanging on the wall over Victor's desk.

Loyalty and preservation of a unified party are important to Jules. He would welcome this approach extending to the whole country. Narrowing down the areas of differences between the political parties and building a national consensus will fulfill Jules's dreams.

"Our visions for the development of the country are not so far apart," Jules says to Victor.

"Maybe for you and I but not your leader." Victor turns away. A bitterness clouds his voice. "I have nothing in common with that man."

"That is not what he told me."

"His word is no good."

Jules's aim is to protect his leader and be an ambassador for the principles of the MNP. He is self-confident, direct, and persistent. He knows Karl expects success.

"I think he makes sense," claims Jules.

"What exactly is he proposing?"

"He wants you to join him."

"Abandon my party?" Victor asks.

"Not exactly."

"Explain."

"You can bring over any of your members you wish."

"I admire his boldness."

"How do you mean?"

"Isn't he aware that he is losing the election?"

"Where do you get your information?"

"Please inform him. He's losing."

Jules is careful not to open himself up to Victor, but he admires the man's self-confidence and calm. He's open rather than controlling.

"He thinks the two of you can combine forces to form a national unity party."

"How well do you know Karl?"

"I have been with him for ten years."

"I knew him before you."

"He has changed. He is more accommodating."

"He is incapable of change. He sees only numbers. His plan is to subtract members from my party to add to his."

Jules knows Victor as competent and trustworthy, and at this point, Jules feels free to express his feelings without conceding his political position or being considered weak.

"I shall convey your message," Jules surrenders. "By the way, did your general secretary tell you he will resign from your party and join us?"

"No."

"Keep your eyes open," Jules says.

***

Richard is meeting with Colonel Lester Bynoe at the embassy.

"Tell me how you plan to handle it," Richard says.

"Here is the plan," Colonel Bynoe outlines. "We will send two undercover men to rattle Milosevic. He will run. When he runs, he is yours!"

"Fine by me," Richard responds. "I don't care how we get him, once he's in our hands."

"Consider this settled?"

"Agreed."

This is the reason he loves doing business with the colonel. Brief, decisive, and to the point. Military style. Where there is doubt, the colonel will tell you straight away, "This will not work."

Colonel Bynoe always wants to ensure that the correct procedures are followed.

Richard appreciates his maturity. At forty-five, he looked more like sixty-five. The close-cropped, thick, dark hair was already showing signs of gray. As an embassy representative, he was stuck in colonial suits most of the time. He envied the colonel's Nehru neck linen or cotton shirts and plain-colored trousers or jeans.

In their dealings, Richard found the man to be a friendly and even lovable person. He associates with everyone and does not discriminate based on class. He loves calypso music and introduced Richard to his favorite singer, the Mighty Sparrow, the calypso king of the world.

Early in their relationship, Richard realized the man is a perfectionist. Self-disciplined and principled in everything he does. He is emotionally controlled and believes there's a right way to do things and a wrong way. He wants to do it the right way.

His standards are high. As a people person, he values relationships. He gets involved with causes to help people. Once he gets close to someone, they become his lifelong concern and so do their children and grandchildren.

A stickler for rights, he doggedly fights for the best results.

Whenever he and Richard worked together, the colonel was always cognizant of their goals and was self-reliant, organized, and punctual. He claims that with every task they accomplish, they take the world closer to perfection.

"How things looking for the boss?" Colonel Bynoe asks.

"Crappy."

"Truly?"

"Yeah, he cannot get away from that last one."

"You believe he should push back the date for the elections?"

"He has no choice but to go ahead with it." Richard steps away from the desk. "Half of his current ministers are distancing themselves from him and his dirty ways."

Richard knows Colonel Bynoe to be clear-minded and objective. There was no formal training for the position he held. One had to rely on a series of skills developed during working life and the application and modification of academic study in a range of subjects. Underlying this is the strength, tenacity, willpower, and courage only developed during service in the military.

"What are his chances of winning the election?"

"He will lose." Richard stops short of the colonel. "We will not be supporting him."

"It's that serious?"

"He is damaged goods."

"That's not what he thinks." The colonel levels Richard's stare. "He feels everything will be all right."

"He thinks his mother's witchcraft will save him." Richard walks to the door. "He is a self-centered, stupid man."

Bynoe's shoulders droop. He has a passion for ensuring all his engagement and assignments turn out correctly, but he is worried. All along, he has believed that whatever the circumstances, the party can still succeed if everyone involved acts correctly.

Errors and loss of control are not in his arsenal. Richard knows, when the elections are over, Bynoe will understand the impossibility of attaining perfection.

Richard smiles. The colonel will realize that the country is complicated, unstable, and unpredictable, and that's fine.

The colonel stands to leave and smiles for the first time during the meeting. "I hope he takes me to the obeah man next time around. I will need plenty of obeah to help him over the next few weeks."

Richard laughs.

The colonel leaves the office.

***

Errol skips excitedly to the main office to meet his writers.

"Gather round, people. Gather round. We got the scoop."

"Boss, relax," one journalist says. "Don't be anxious."

"Anxious. Wait until you hear it."

"Tell us."

"We will be running two separate stories on the same topic," Errol says, pausing. "No, strike that, four stories. We need an exclusive on the upcoming elections. Purely on the election. Another one on the opposition's perspective of the elections and what they consider their chances to be."

"Should we include random people's views?"

"That's the third story. The fourth will be on Ingrid Frank and Jules Bourne. They will not be running the next election."

"Did you check the political scientist's opinion polls?"

"Wait, this is story number five."

"This will be an election paper?"

"Is that a problem?"

"No, I am thinking aloud."

"Get to work, people. Everything must be in the next issue. We have the exclusive. We have the lead on the others. Let's milk it. Get going!"

Errol exits the building, leaving the journalists discussing his demands.

***

Karl storms into the Cabinet room. He is late and in a vicious mood. He sits and addresses them at once.

"Although you have heard it by now, let me clarify. I don't know why I am singling you out for special treatment, when frankly, none of you deserve it. I must tell you the truth. Ten of you will not be selected to run in the next election. You have not defended me during the recent attacks on me. You didn't put your narrow self-interest ahead of the party, government, or the country.

"Don't think you're hurting me. I have my businesses and my money. I don't need this. I decided to help this country. I could have been working in the United States for ten times my current salary. You cannot spite me. Look at me. Fit, healthy, and strong. I can go on forever. Many of you cannot even climb a hill.

"My slate will be announced soon."

He storms out of the room.

Diana and Jules stay in the Cabinet room after the others leave.

"So, you and I are getting the chop," Diana says.

"I picked up that vibe. He said ten of us," Jules says blandly.

"He can't drop me." Diana is blunt.

"What do you mean?"

"Put another way, he cannot afford to drop me. I will make sure of that."

"What do you have in mind?"

"He cannot resist me. He will want me, and I am not for free."

"What should I do?" Jules asks Diana.

"Stop dropping money for him."

"How you know that?"

"He told me."

"Why did he say this?"

"You men." She laughs. "When you want a woman, you will spill your guts. I hid twenty thousand dollars away for him."

"I should blackmail him?" Jules is confused.

"Approach him and let him have it straight. He drops you. You give him to the dogs."

Diana walks out of the room, leaving Jules stunned.

***

Cathy walks toward the secretary in the front office.

"Go ahead. He is expecting you," the man says without looking up. He continues to enter data with a computer keyboard.

She walks through the door behind the man and closes it.

"Tell me about section 84.8 of the constitution." The voice booms from the kitchenette.

"I can't quote it, but I am able to explain the section," she says.

"Why were certain positions enshrined in the constitution?"

"For protection of the position, I guess," she answers.

"You were the highest-ranking public officer, and you're guessing."

"I haven't read the constitution in a while," she claims.

The owner of the voice emerges from the kitchenette. A tall light brown man in his seventies, his gray hair short and curly. He smiles showing a perfect set of well-fitted white implants. He carries an empty glass in one hand and a plate of assorted crackers and cheese in the other. Slightly bent, he walks to his desk and sits. He ushers her to sit.

"The only document that can save you and you haven't read it?"

She'd heard about F. M. Smith QC, but it's her first meeting with him. He had drafted the constitution of Mabuya leading up to the island gaining independence from Great Britain. As a prominent lawyer, he accompanied the then prime minister to London to negotiate independence.

"It didn't cross my mind," she says.

"There is a copy in front of you. Read," he demands. "I have my copy."

She takes the document from the desk and begins reading. He dips into his drawer and pulls out a bottle of local bush rum, pouring a shot into a glass. He follows the rum with a sip of water from a nearby bottle.

Smith munches from his plate, while she reads.

Then he goes to the washroom. She hears him piss, wash his hands, and brush his teeth before returning to his desk.

"I see what you mean," she says.

"Who is advising the prime minister?" he asks. "It should be you as Cabinet secretary."

"I think it's based on his feelings," she claims.

"Having refreshed your memory on your constitutional position, how do you evaluate your case?" he asks.

"I think my removal is unconstitutional," she says.

"Talk to me." He leans forward grinning wickedly.

"I see that the governor general erred in transferring me to an unknown post and leaving the Public Service Commission to find somewhere to place me," she explains.

"What else?"

"I think the transfer ends my appointment as secretary to the Cabinet," she says.

"Now you are talking," he says, sitting back in the chair. "The post they intended to transfer you to did not exist. Even if it existed, it cannot be equivalent to the post you held. The creation of the post is a reorganization. This is, in effect, a retirement. We will argue you are entitled to pension and retirement benefits as if you had attained the compulsory retirement age and all other damages and costs the court may order."

"Mr. Smith, I concur."

"Let us file." He grins.

***

Michelle and Kenny are in the living room watching television news in which Karl is explaining his reason for calling an early election.

"Why did he have to do that?" Michelle asks.

"He had no choice, baby," Kenny answers

"Don't *baby* me. I am not your baby."

"No difference, you are my brother's baby."

"I asked why he is calling elections eighteen months early?"

"They are not pulling their weight."

"Why should they when he is so blasted deceitful? He treats these people like dogs."

"He treats you that way?"

"I have faith, Kenny Boy, I have faith. He cannot move my faith."

"So why don't you just divorce him?"

"Why should I? We made a vow, till death do us part, in sickness and in health."

"Even if you unhappy?"

"I don't care. I am worried that the Viagra might kill him or he might contract HIV or something. My happiness is in my mind, and he has never been able to penetrate that."

"What kind of woman are you?"

"You just wondering? Your brother knows me. He knows my strength."

"Divorce the man and let him live his life."

"Mark my words tonight, Kenny. He will lose this election. When he does, he will come crying on my shoulder."

"Wishful thinking."

Michelle returns her attention to Karl ending his speech.

***

Karl rolls out of Diana's bed and starts to dress. She pulls the sheet around her body and stares at him.

"The rumor is you plan to drop me from the team," she says.

Karl pulls on his sock and turns to face her.

"Where did you get that shit?"

"I have my sources." She smiles.

"That is not true."

"Fine. I had to hear it coming from you."

"Darling, don't let people thief your head and drive a wedge between us. Me and you good."

"Why don't you resign?" she asks.

"Why should I?"

"You are not a spring chicken anymore," she claims.

"Didn't I do well tonight?"

"You should be thankful. Many men in their thirties cannot get an erection," she says.

"They should exercise and watch their diet," he boasts.

"Some people are sick."

"Well, I am not."

"You need to relax, enjoy the rest of your life."

"Who should I hand over to?"

"Jules."

"Jules has no ambition, and he is not educated enough," Karl says.

"He has a bachelor's degree, Karl."

"He is good at what he does. Run errands."

She shakes her head as Karl finishes dressing and leaves the room.

***

The police constable on diary at the police station looks up to see Colonel Bynoe standing over him. He fidgets but remains seated.

"Do you have Ras in there?" the colonel asks.

"I cannot tell you that."

"Find somebody who can."

"Who are you?"

Colonel Bynoe pulls out his cell phone and speed dials a number.

"I am in front of the diarist," the colonel is direct.

With minutes, the sergeant walks out to the front desk and jumps to full attention, saluting Colonel Bynoe.

"How can I assist you, Colonel?"

Copying the sergeant's actions, the police constable also jumps to full attention, saluting Colonel Bynoe, who ignores him.

"Do you have a young man called Ras held here?"

"Ras is in there, but he isn't young. He is a senior citizen."

"He is young in his heart. How long you had him here?"

"From yesterday, sir."

"Did he see a doctor?"

"No, sir."

"Take him to the hospital immediately. Advise the hospital to release him as soon as they are through with him."

"I am on it, sir."

"Thank you, Sarge."

This time the constable stands at attention as Colonel Bynoe turns and walks out of the police station.

The colonel sits in his vehicle outside the station until they leave with Ras. He wonders if he has underestimated Karl's propensity to deceive. His level of honesty might not allow him to comprehend Karl's style and deception. It can be an exercise in futility attempting to predict or discern the inner workings of Karl's devious mind. Double-dealing and double-crossing get the straight-shooting colonel furious. He deals with everyone on an open, clear basis.

His fear is that the tricks and deceit of Karl would ruin the party and destroy the government. This is hard to discuss with anyone. Even Jules. He knows that Jules handles many of Karl's darkest transactions including monies collected on behalf of the party and never handed in to the organization.

Colonel Bynoe starts his car and eases out of the police station yard, wondering how to influence the progress of his government and party going forward, beyond the election.

Increasingly, Karl has become a liability to the progress of the country. As a social animal, the colonel loves to hang out by small bars with his friends. As a former sportsman, he enjoys a good game of cricket, football, and other athletics. His nose is on the ground, and recent sniffs have detected sourness among the population. Karl has lost ground.

The colonel eases the car onto the main road.

He serves the prime minster loyally. His duties range from the spectacular to the mundane. Today's mission to release Ras left him with more questions than answers. Why was he picked up in the first place? Why send him, a high-ranking official, to free Ras? Any lawyer could have done so. Was he being used? Manipulated? Belittled?

Colonel Bynoe shakes the thought out of his head and focuses on the traffic ahead.

***

Karl is sipping a cup of tea at the dining table when Swaggart pokes his head around the doorway.

"I tried to stop him, but he says he cannot sleep if he does not talk to you."

"Who is that?"

"Minister Bourne."

"Let him come in. I hope it's important at this late hour."

Swaggart withdraws his head, and Jules comes into the room sweating and breathing hard.

"What happen?" Karl asks. "You have an emergency?"

"Ah hear ah ain't running again."

"Where you hear dat from?"

"Good solid grounds."

"The team has not been selected," Karl claims.

"That's what I find strange," Jules says.

"Come on, a man with your experience, you are falling for rumors man."

Jules realizes he has lost control. He's never spoken to Karl like this before. He has always been in command of his actions, purposeful and discreet. He believes in the team and counts on the leader to bring home the win.

He gets things done without complications, but now he wonders about Karl. Is Karl taking him for granted? Will he spend the rest of his life feeding off Karl's crumbs? Never fulfilling his own dreams and ambitions? Is he prepared to go down with Karl's sinking ship?

"What is your plan for me when we win?"

"I haven't thought about that yet," Karl stutters.

"Knowing you, this cannot be true."

"Come on, Jules." Karl grins. "Would I lie to you?"

Jules thinks, *Yes, you would.* On his part, he has been straight, upfront, and frank in his dealings with Karl. In his mind, he is confident that his contributions thus far have strengthened the MNP and Mabuya.

Assessing his own weakness, Jules admits there are times when he ignores the team and only considers Karl's interests. High-handedness and lack of empowerment have cost him the respect of his comrades.

He hates losing control. The team must contribute. Others must perform their roles. Stand up for themselves. Thoughts bounce against one another in his mind.

"I expect you to be truthful," Jules admits.

"In that case you have nothing to worry about," Karl says.

Jules feels patronized. Karl is attempting to placate him. Others are jealous of his relationship with Karl and have made attempts to come between them. Over the years he has been uncomfortable with their close relationship. In this moment he feels the distance.

Jules bows his head in shame, looking at the floor questioningly.

"Doh let nobody fool you," Karl says calmly.

"I had to come straight to you. I had to get it off my chest. I went home but I just could not sleep."

He has been too dependent on Karl. Karl makes the decisions. He follows the orders. The leader does the thinking; he executes. He has forgotten what it is like to make decisions and follow through with the implementation.

Listening to Karl's hollow assurances, Jules realizes his dependency. He is addicted to Karl. He has to believe him.

"Of course. You did the right thing coming here."

Karl coaxes Jules to the door.

***

Michelle is sitting at a computer workstation on one side of the bedroom. She looks at the screen and writes in her notebook: *HSBC – $1.2M. BNS – $2.3M. SUISSE – $5.4M. CHASE – $4.5M.* She powers off the laptop and tears the page from her notebook, placing it between the pages of her Bible.

She stares at the dark screen and caresses the cover of the Bible. At the end of the day, she knows this will be the reason for Karl's return to her. He needs her but needs the money more.

She remembers the first time he used her to hide his money from the authorities. They were on their way to Mabuya Island and had stopped off on Belle Isle to meet with his CIA handlers. A delegation led by Victor came over from Mabuya Island to join the meeting to work on the formation of a US-supported government in Mabuya.

Karl entered their cottage that night sweating and breathing heavily. She watched him fling his shoes off and run into her arms clutching a canvas bag.

"You have to handle this," he said.

"What is it?" she asked.

"You open it and deal with it." He dropped the bag on the ground, stripped, and headed to the bathroom.

She opened the bag to reveal a stash of neatly packed US dollar bills. She closed it.

He emerged from the bathroom in a set of clean boxers and headed toward the bed.

"Not so fast. You have some explaining to do," she said.

"What do you want to know?"

"Where did this money come from? Why did they give it to you?"

"Everyone at the meeting got their share. It's for the political campaign. You might not like it, but it's for the good of the country."

"Where did the money come from, Karl?"

"Our American friends."

"Why didn't they wire the funds to you?"

"Impossible."

"Why?"

"It is not clean money."

Michelle walked away from the bed to sit on a desk chair at the writing table. Karl was on the edge of the bed, propping up his head with his hand.

"You've got to explain, and I am not busy."

"Ollie North, CIA controller for the Western Hemisphere, came up with a plan. He realized millions of dollars are seized every year by the CIA in counterterrorism and anti-narcotics operations. This money cannot be repatriated to the United States or filtered into the banking system. He decided to use that cash to finance parties like ours."

"What do you mean 'parties like yours'?"

"Analyze our current situation. We are stepping into the unknown. Most of us have not set foot on the island in twenty years. The party is made up of five different factions. Under normal circumstances this collection of men would never sit in the same room. The CIA brought us together for the common good of the nation. When we hit the ground in Mabuya, we will need cash. This will be an expensive campaign."

"I am your mule."

He moves to kneel at her feet.

"This is our big break. I am not spending half of this money on the campaign. I will carry some, you will carry a portion, and the remainder you will bank here in your name. Everybody knows your parents are rich. It will seem that they gave you some money."

She looks at him, laying her hand on his shoulder.

"Karl, it is said no leader starts off with the intention of being corrupt. It starts with one small first step toward dishonesty—the initial small favor, for the good of the country and the wider cause. I am sure that as the election campaign progresses, Ollie will pump more money in. By that time you guys will not be able to turn back. You will be on a downward trajectory, on the slippery slope to moral decadence. The pull toward power and money has no end. It is one long never-ending rope to oblivion."

"Darling, do you always have to be so dramatic? I know when to stop."

She pushes Karl away and walks to the glass door to the verandah, then turns to face him. He sits on her chair.

"There is nowhere to stop on that road. Once you take it, you're on it to the end."

"Where is all this philosophy coming from suddenly? We've done things that were not legitimate before."

"This is different. This is where you propose to me 'let's get on cocaine.' It's addictive."

"It's all about control. We are going to do this once," Karl begs.

"Then we stop?"

"Certainly. You have my word."

"As your wife I will support you. I will need to talk to the Lord in prayer."

"Do that." He smiles.

"Wait, did anybody refuse the money?"

"There was one man who didn't want to join the alliance. He said he had not yet decided on entering politics. Ollie asked him why. He claimed he had a mortgage on his house and car. They asked him how much. The man tells them fifty thousand dollars. Ollie counted out one hundred thousand dollars and gave it to him. That guy never spoke for the rest of the day."

"Karl, this is the problem. This is addictive and spreads like a disease. In the beginning, each member weighs his personal position. As time goes by, members look at the benefits afforded to others and compare their advancement in life. They also assess the likelihood of their activities going public and public reaction to their behavior. At some point, the team becomes numb to the transactions, then they no longer take notice of the frequency. The members become rotten. The CIA has won."

"You sound like a communist."

"If that's what you call it."

"A prophecy of doom and gloom."

"This is the hypocrisy of you fellas. You talk of democracy and opposition. As soon as someone opposes your position, you pounce on them and stick labels. You don't tolerate divergent views, other voices are stifled, and one group of people dominates the party in power as the party in opposition."

Karl stands.

"I am going to bed. When you pray, look at the bigger picture. We are trying to restore democracy to a country ruled by communists. It is our duty to do all within our power to ensure that they never rise again. I will be prime minister soon, and you will be there as the wife of the prime minister."

"You are so full of yourself." Michelle grimaces.

She reopens the Bible and reads the verse where she had placed the loose notebook page.

The wealth of the rich is his fortified city; in his imagination it is like a high wall.

—Proverbs 18:11

***

Karl is seated between Diana James, the commissioner of police, and other elite members of the Mabuya Police Force at a ceremony to promote twenty officers to higher rank. Colonel Lester Bynoe is at the podium chairing the ceremony.

"Officers, you are the final twenty chosen for promotion by the commissioner and his team," Colonel Bynoe announces.

"Those who did not make it this time, don't despair. You will have another opportunity next year. Work harder, be dedicated and determined, and you will move up the ranks of the Mabuya Police Force.

"Officers, Prime Minister Karl Stone, our minister of national security is here today. I will invite him to make a few remarks at this time so that he can be on his way. He is a busy man."

"Prime Minister."

He waits for Karl to reach the podium before taking his seat.

Karl addresses the crowd, "Members of the Cabinet, commissioner of police, members of the police general staff, police officers. As the colonel pointed out, my remarks will be brief. On my way here today, I tried to formulate and capture the essence of police work and the increased responsibility being placed on your shoulders with this promotion.

"The first thing to note is that you are now joining a higher rank of an elite group of men and women whose purpose is to help people and provide a service to the nation. You are the first stop for people attempting to get satisfaction when they feel they have been wronged.

"You must investigate disputes since the court may require you to present evidence. You are an asset to our justice system. Take heed.

"I welcome you to your new ranks. You have worked hard for it. You deserve it."

Swaggart is standing off to one side of the podium. He looks to the sky, mutters to himself, and rolls his eyes.

"I expect you to do your duties with skill and aptitude. They may not tell you to your face, but people respect you, and they are thankful for the job you do every day."

Swaggart is increasingly uneasy and restive.

"I want to leave you with an important message today. Always remember, with greater power comes greater responsibility. The higher you climb in the Mabuya Police Force, the more is expected of you. Thank you."

Karl steps away from the podium, waves to the commissioner and others, and walks to the exit. Swaggart follows.

They stride across the netball court and enter Karl's official vehicle.

"Boss, can I ask you something?"

"Of course, Swaggart. Of course."

"What do you have to do to get a promotion?"

"Well, like I explained, hard work, dedication, service, and being helpful to people."

"Okay, boss."

They drive along quietly for some time before Karl looks slightly troubled.

"Swaggart, why did you ask me that?"

"Nuttin'."

"Swaggart, do not try to be cute with me. Something is on your mind."

"Me. How come I was not promoted? You know I am only a corporal, right?"

"You. I didn't know you wanted a promotion. I thought you were happy where you are." Silence engulfs the vehicle as they continue to drive.

***

Karl squats on a stool at a table in an old garage shed with three other men playing dominoes. Swaggart and another security guard take up strategic positions within the garage. A few people are milling around. Some are eating and drinking, others are in private conversations, while a few are around the table watching the game.

Jimmy, Swaggart's brother, is Karl's partner, and he poses with a double six-piece. Karl looks at him suspiciously.

Karl surveys Jimmy over his domino hand. He knows the man could not keep a job. Years ago, he'd vowed to award him petty construction contracts at Swaggart's insistence. He learned of the man's gambling and debts through police wiretapping and a barrage of court cases. Soon, the reports emerged in the media, and the story became public. Swaggart claimed he didn't know of his brother's weakness.

After a few contracts, the man surrendered. Debt from his compulsive gambling had overwhelmed him.

Karl had suggested to Swaggart that they seek help for Jimmy's gambling problem.

Jimmy checks his dominoes and asks for a rum and Coke.

Swaggart mixes the drink and passes it to his brother.

Jimmy sips the drink.

"You got it locked, man. You know my mix."

"You're welcome," Swaggart says.

"Boss, did you work on the thing for me?" Jimmy asks.

"What was it again?" Karl asks.

The man next to Jimmy plays his domino, then Karl plays.

"The land," Jimmy reminds him.

"Oh. Yeah, man. That's done. Check Jules," Karl answers.

"Okay, boss. I knew you would not fail me."

"Yes, man, I handled it as soon as you told me," Karl claims.

The other man at the table plays, and it's Jimmy's turn.

"Pass," Jimmy says.

"Mr. Jimmy, you have one blasted piece of six and you just pose with it." Karl is getting angry.

"Double six. Ah ain't keeping it in my hand." Jimmy is sure of himself.

"How many times do I have to teach you all how to play this game?" Karl asks.

"Well, boss, you doh must get so hot." Jimmy tries to calm Karl.

The men play another round, and Jimmy passes again. This time Karl passes too.

"Now you pass me. This is the kinda blasted shit I can't take!" Karl yells at Jimmy.

The game goes two more rounds, and the other team gains two points, winning both ends of the board. Karl is visibly upset.

"Boss, it's only a game. We are here to have fun and relax." Jimmy smiles.

"And on top of that, I have to sit here and take a crappy lecture from you," Karl shouts.

"Boss, I didn't mean…" Jimmy stutters.

"I am out of here, man. I don't need this shit." Karl get up, slams his dominoes on the table, and storms out of the shed. Swaggart and the other security guard run to keep pace with him.

Karl climbs into the rear of the vehicle, whips out his phone, and speed-dials a number.

"Jules, you remember that thing I asked you to work on for Jimmy? Yes, the land. Cancel it. Cancel every shit. He is too damn disrespectful."

Karl cuts off the conversation and leans back for the short ride home.

CHAPTER TEN

The ninja slides across the yard silently. He covers the yard in seconds, jumps the verandah, and sprints to the front door. He picks the lock, enters the living room, and walks briskly over to the kitchen. He brazenly opens the refrigerator, pulls out a beer, opens it, and starts drinking.

Karl is in bed next to Michelle. He is tossing and turning uncomfortably. He is dreaming about a cricket match in a rural area with spectators from surrounding villages. Karl is sixteen years old and running in to bowl. The crowd boos and heckles him. Ras is at the forefront of the jeering.

"Move you ass dey. You can't bowl and you can't bat."

Karl loses concentration, breaks his step, turns, and goes back to his mark. He grips the ball, ready to deliver his spin bowling. Ras is in front of him again, shaking and prancing and shouting to his face with the crowd spurring him on.

"You ah pussy. You can't captain the team. You full ah shit."

Karl loses concentration and is forced to stop. He looks around at the crowd. Most of them are his friends from school and their parents. He is overwhelmed by their lack of solidarity.

He pushes the ball into his pocket and walks to the sidelines to gather his belongings. He takes his personal effects, including the box of cricket balls, and walks away from the crowd with his chin held high and his mouth stretched resolutely.

"Play without my flipping balls," Karl says to the players.

In his sleep, Karl shivers slightly with a smirk on his face.

In the kitchen, the ninja finishes the beer and continues his mission. He stealthily moves to the bottom of the stairs leading to the master bedroom and glides to the top. He opens the bedroom door and moves toward the bed.

He draws a short sword and approaches Karl and Michelle where they lie on the bed. He comes close to Karl and lifts the sword high in the air to execute his mission and suddenly freezes.

He lowers the sword, sheathes it, and retreats the way he came.

Michelle wakes up, looking around puzzled. She shakes Karl.

He looks at her groggily. Instinctively, he checks the time on his clock nearby. It's 2:00 a.m.

"Were you talking to somebody?" Michelle asks.

"I had this awful dream," Karl says.

"About what?"

"I don't remember it now. But it was very confusing."

"Do you recall anything at all?" Michelle asks.

"No. Let's go back to bed. I want to get up just now," Karl says.

"Okay."

Karl tries to get back to sleep.

Michelle remains wide awake thinking of a world where she knows things but cannot decipher what she knows.

***

The ninja moves around the back of the house and into the garage, where several vehicles are parked. He stoops behind an SUV and starts to remove his ninjutsu outfit. He takes off the outer wear, revealing a pair of shorts and T-shirt. He stuffs the suit into a bag, opens the trunk of a vehicle, and tosses the bag inside, closing the trunk.

The ninja exhales audibly as he sees his darkened face in the SUV's mirror. It is Swaggart. He leans on the trunk.

"You not worth it," he whispers.

***

Rita and Karl are sitting across the table from Dr. Blunt.

"Doc, my son has a problem sleeping in the night."

"What is the problem?"

"I think somebody is dipping their hand in his blood, and I told him so."

"Well, why don't you let him speak for himself?" the doctor suggests.

Rita, a defensive cat, stiffens.

"Tell him, Karl."

Dr. Blunt switches his attention to Karl.

"I am having weird dreams, and I have trouble getting a full night's sleep."

"Do you wake up fighting?"

"Yes. Tense, sweating, and sometimes trading punches."

"How long has this been happening?"

"A long time. Months. Honestly, Doc, it's been years."

"Are you on any medication?"

"Only blood pressure."

"Were you advised of any side effects? Any related changes?"

"No."

"This is what we will do."

Dr. Blunt writes Karl a prescription.

"Within the next few days, check yourself into a private lab. The procedure will not exceed an hour."

Dr. Blunt tears the paper from his pad.

"Give this to them. They will carry out the tests, and I will let you know when we have the results."

"Thank you, Doc," Karl says.

"Thanks, Doc," Rita echoes.

"Doc, how much do I owe you?"

"Tell me. How could I charge the prime minister? That's nothing. Get well."

"I am grateful. Do not hesitate to call me."

Karl hands Dr. Blunt a calling card.

"This has my personal number."

Rita and Karl exit the office.

***

Diana is at Royal Mabuyan Hotel having breakfast with Richard. Their seats face each other but they make sure that they can see the calm blue Caribbean Sea. The sun is rising and creating glittering shadows across the surface of the lagoon. A scattering of fishing boats, yachts, and small cabin cruisers litter the bay.

"Why do I have work?" Richard asks.

"What do you mean?" says Diana.

"This setting. This view. I can enjoy it for the entire day. Just relaxing and sipping on scotch."

"But you can. No one will be running after you. People think you are a retiree."

"You're right. Been here too goddamn long."

"Maybe you should work for the party in the next election. Replace me."

"Very funny. If I had to endure working under Karl, I would shoot his ass."

"You would. He's a piece of work."

"We are sick of him and his shit."

"He is so evil."

"We will not overthrow him, but our relationship is finished."

"Is he aware of that?"

"I told him, Diana. I told him."

"He pretends not to know."

"You know he is a great pretender."

"Richard, he feels someone wants to kill him. Did he tell you?"

"He has wronged so many people, he won't know who wants to kill him."

"He can't sleep at night, he claims. It's frightening."

"Let him stew in his own sauce. My people will not save him."

"Richard, I want to campaign against him."

"Great. We will finance you. Just tell me what you need."

"I know I can count on you, my husband."

He smiles. "Yes, wifey."

The waitress brings their breakfast, which they attack with gusto.

***

Errol is pacing the floor of his newsroom office clutching a set of papers. He flicks through the papers rapidly but pays attention to the contents of each page.

"I want to suggest two pages. Front and back. What do you guys think?"

he asks.

"As soon as you tell us the story," a journalist says.

"My mistake. Thought you guys knew. The news is everywhere."

"Well?"

"Minister Diana James is fed up with Karl. He has broken his promises to her, and she is pissed off and talking."

"We heard that, but is it true?"

"My source is the horse's mouth."

"Let's have it."

"Front page. *He is a little boy*. She accuses him of being childish. Extremely jealous and conniving. He conspires for months until he gets you. She gave the example of a man who worked at her ministry and had a crush on her; within months the man was forced to retire from public service and leave the country."

"Back page?"

"Diana is bitter. She wants more from her relationship with Karl and the party. Even if she runs for election, she won't be representing his party."

Errol flicks through the stack of papers.

"Listen," he tells his staff. "She describes him as a man who knows how to get people to follow him. He promises the world but never delivers. Karl grants favors to the people near him to keep them loyal. Persuades them that he has this great vision for the future, while he knows this to be untrue. He uses people to make himself acceptable to society.

"As the leader of the party, he concentrates on adding members to its ranks. That is his measure of success. Then he pushes the party program and inspires urgency toward achieving goals that only he sets.

"This man maintains party loyalty by playing members against one another. New ideas are not tolerated. He has not appointed a successor."

Errol bypasses a few pages, sips water, and continues.

"Karl is an anxious and moody man, likely to explode without warning. His greatest fear is loss of control. He enjoys the trappings of power and the manipulation of people that goes with it. She thinks that without power, his social functioning will be destroyed.

"She says he recently exploded, cursing her without reason. Accusing her of being lazy and ungrateful. His aggression rattled her. He smashed the glass he was drinking from into the wall and told her to get out of his sight. The man has a short fuse.

"Then, he calls her that night wanting to visit because he is depressed. She finds it difficult to understand the change from explosive aggression to manic depression within hours. Here is a man who is friendly and approachable one minute, then morphs into an unpleasant, irritable, and apprehensive being within seconds.

"Her final insult relates to his ability to lose interest in sex. One minute they are making love; the next minute he loses interest. He loses pleasure just as fast as he acquires it. She thinks that the loss of enjoyment is the manifestation of his depression.

"The man cannot sleep at night. He jumps up with fear, rough breathing, and sweating. He thinks someone wants to kill him. No one can comfort him during those moments. This makes him irritable and flustered for the whole day."

Errol lowers the document.

"I am not going to ask you the obvious," a reporter says.

"My source is ironclad, tight, secure. What should we do, guys?" Errol responds.

"Let's hit the road. Run with it. Back and front pages."

"Get on it then."

Errol returns to his office.

The staff scrambles back to their workstations.

***

Yellow is standing behind the bar dressed in black. Four other customers wearing black and white are seated scattered around.

"He had a good turnout," one customer says.

"Yes, there was good support for him." Yellow dabs his eyes with a handkerchief.

"I am shocked you closed the bar and came," another customer says.

"You know I don't fancy funerals. Ras was me boy. Many times, he and I will be alone in the shop. We discuss every subject, including his frustrations with Karl," Yellow says.

"May his soul rest in peace," a woman says.

"This round is on the house. I will fill up everybody," Yellow announces.

He hands out the drinks, then raises his glass in the air.

"For Ras," a customer says.

"For Ras," Yellow and the others echo. They empty their glasses.

"Did they say how he died?" a customer asks.

"Not a word." Yellow sniffles and dabs his eyes. "We will never know. I heard they were moving him from the police station to the hospital to see a doctor. He died on his way to the hospital."

"Did they say what killed him?" the customer asks.

"Heart failure," Yellow says.

"That is Ras. He was so scared of the police; seeing was enough to make his heart fail," a customer says.

"I am voting against Karl," Yellow says.

"We voting with you, Yellow. All ah we is one," one man says.

"Karl losing his mind, yes. This is too much," another adds.

"What is the latest? How the newspapers say the election looking?" a woman asks.

Yellow pulls the newspaper from under the counter and reads aloud.

Dictatorship and corruption allegations dog the Mabuyan National Party (MNP) as they enter the upcoming elections. In the latest opinion polls, people show concern about the highhandedness and singularity of Prime Minister Karl Stone. When asked, 80 percent of respondents say that dictatorship and corruption will influence their vote against the MNP in the next election.

Seventy percent of voters prefer the style of leadership portrayed by Victor Calliste, head of the opposition Mabuyan Democratic Movement (MDM). Fifteen years ago, the MDM, under the leadership of James Boca, lost the elections to the MNP following corruption allegations and mishandling of the economy.

Though persons interviewed still have reservations about the MDM from that time in power, they claim they will give the party another chance.

Grumblings from within the MNP express unhappiness with PM Stone's leadership. They say the politics of the country will only change with genuine reform at the highest level. The people want to curtail the power of the prime minister, who they say has become a "Ground God," using favoritism dictating the lives of his ministers and the population. PM Stone has created a club of yes-men around him who support all his wrongdoing.

The Americans own evidence showing Stone taking a bribe from a known criminal element wanted by the US government. In any other country, Prime Minister Stone would be brought before the relevant authorities to answer the allegations.

In addition, the poll shows that the MNP machinery is not election-ready in several constituencies. The party hasn't convinced voters of its plans and programs—in particular, its plan to create jobs and stem the rising unemployment in the country.

Overall, polls have the MNP losing 30 percent of its support from the last election.

***

Karl and executive members of the MNP are gathered at the party headquarters.

Jules is the chairman for this special meeting.

"Good day, members, and thank you for coming," he says. "I will open the floor for a member to lead us in a word of prayer." He surveys the room. "Any takers?"

A member stands.

"Let us all stand."

Everyone gets up.

"Lord, as we gather to talk the business of this party, we call upon you to help us in our discussions. We call upon you, Lord, to help us make the right decisions. Lord, we thank you for being there for us over the years and showing us the way.

"Lord, we thank you for giving us our political leader, Karl Stone. We ask that you keep him in good health and strength. We thank you, Lord. Amen."

Everyone sits.

"Our political leader has called this meeting to discuss the political situation. Wasting no time, I will let him explain to you the only item on the agenda today."

Jules looks around the room before focusing on Karl.

"Members, I invite our political leader to speak to you."

Karl remains seated.

"Good day, members. Once again, let me thank you for coming here despite the short notice. As Brother Jules stated, we are here to talk about one thing. The upcoming elections. And I have only one goal: to win.

"Many of you are shaky right now. You have joined with others in saying and thinking wicked things. You think I must give up, abandon what I have worked hard for. Just walk away. You believe I have done something wrong, that Karl must go. Karl must step aside for somebody else.

"I have news for you. Those who are going around spreading these rumors and making statements, tell dem I ain't going, no way. Nobody go run me. Ah hanging on as strong as ah monkey's tail. I have fought better than dem and won. I will win again. Go out there; secure your seats. Mine is safe.

"The little boy running against me is a fool. What is his name? I hear they call him Suzie or Susan, or something like that. In my constituency, I'm still paying bills left by the girl who ran in the last election."

Karl leans forward, his eyes blazing with anger and rage. He looks squarely at each member in the room, momentarily pausing to stare into each one's eyes and holding the contact before moving to the next.

"This is my message to you guys. I have called the election; you cannot change that. They say I call it too early. So be it. They say I was supposed to ask them when to call it. That's my prerogative. The race start. Go out there and do your work. Work with your constituents, secure your seat, and stop worrying.

"I don't even need this politics. You need it more than me. I am doing this to help you. Get off your ass. Increase your election work."

Karl leans back in his chair and exhales. He turns to Jules.

"Jules, meet me in the office."

Karl gets up, saunters to the office, and slams the door behind him. Jules follows him.

In the office, Karl is sipping from a small bottle of water he took from the mini refrigerator in the corner of the room. He tosses a bottle to Jules as he enters the room. Jules catches the bottle.

"You still have skills, guy," Karl says.

"A little. I still have everything in me," Jules replies.

"Only your woman could attest to that," Karl says.

"When you see her, ask her," Jules returns.

"I will, if I can find her," Karl remarks snidely.

"I am not gay," Jules responds stubbornly.

"I have never seen you with a woman."

"I keep my business private."

"That's your prerogative."

Jules changes the direction of the conversation. "So, talk to me."

Karl walks over to stand directly in front of Jules, toe to toe.

"What you collect so far?"

"It is tight. Men are not committing."

"Why?"

"They not sure you will win."

"We need to show dem who is boss."

"What can we do? I spoke to the regular businessmen, the Indians, the Syrians, a few locals around the town and a couple big-time promoters. Same sentiments. They have already started making friends with the opposition.

"I might be going down, but I ain't down yet."

"What do you want me to do?"

"You don't worry. I will send somebody to talk to them. What's the latest with the incoming foreign funding?"

"Some of it is here."

"You didn't tell me."

"I thought you knew."

"How much?"

"I have not checked it yet."

"Check it and bring it to me."

"I will."

"Good night, then."

"Yes, good night."

Jules leaves the room.

Karl picks up the phone and dials Colonel Bynoe's number.

"Do you know of any incident involving a yacht that sailed into the port?" Karl asks.

"Yes," answers Colonel Bynoe.

"What happened?" Karl asks.

"The yacht came in, and the chief immigration officer summoned the captain to his office and gave him thirty minutes to leave."

"Why?"

"He said their clearance papers were not in order. Didn't he report to you?" Colonel Bynoe inquires.

"No. Remove that fool from the post tonight," Karl demands.

"Consider that done," the colonel says.

"And, Colonel, remember, I don't care what nobody says!" Karl barks.

"Understood, sir."

Karl replaces the phone and slams the half-empty bottle of water into the wall.

***

Enveloped in heat, Jules and Colonel Bynoe are talking in the steam room of a hotel. They are naked, except for the white towels wrapped around their waistlines.

"What is your analysis of the present political affairs?" Colonel Bynoe asks.

"The big man has lost his support," Jules says.

"Why do you say that?"

"People who I knew as strong supporters are saying they had enough of him. Not the party but he. They see him as selfish, dishonest, and wicked."

"What does that say for the elections?"

"He is losing."

"Did you tell him that?"

"He didn't ask me."

"Suppose he asks?"

Jules looks at the colonel and pauses.

"Nah. I have nothing to say."

"Aren't you obliged to tell him what you are picking up on the ground?"

"Not everything."

"He is your boss."

"No way."

"I don't understand."

"How well do you know this guy?"

"I work for him. I bring him reports, and he takes them in stride."

"When you bring him reports, what does he do with them?"

"I suppose he studies them and follows the recommendations."

"Name me one. One recommendation of yours that he has followed."

Colonel Bynoe pauses for a long while with a troubled expression on his face.

"Can't say any offhand."

"There is none. He uses his own channel. He implements whatever suits him."

Colonel Bynoe looks taken aback.

"Never saw it that way. But now you mention it, it makes sense."

"He must always look good. The sun, the moon, and the stars shine from his arse. He is cute, he sweet, he can screw any woman he wants, and at seventy-two years old, he has no intention of dying now."

Jules's analysis shakes the colonel. He shifts uncomfortably in the heat.

"How do you cope?"

Jules's eyes fill with tears. "I am the errand boy. I drop his bags of money for him, keep peace in the camp, and tell him what he wants to hear."

"This is serious shit."

"Yes, but people are on to him; he will lose this election."

"How terrible is it?"

"He will be lucky to keep two seats along with his. The opposition will win at least eleven seats."

The colonel forces a smile, which turns into a grimace.

"That is terrible."

"It is a disaster for me. I still have my mother's medical bills to pay."

"Lord help us."

"Lord help him."

The men stand and drop their towels to put on bathing trunks.

The colonel follows Jules to the exit of the steam room and into the bubbling four-person whirlpool.

***

In the cathedral yard, Michelle parks among vehicles belonging to the priests and other laymen. She exits the car and walks around to the front of the cathedral. She strides up the steps and enters a small door behind the altar.

In the confessional booth, she sits facing the priest. Her hands tighten.

"Forgive me, Father, for I have sinned."

"How long has it been since your last confession?"

"Father, it has been over two years since my last confession."

"What brings you here today, my child?"

"Father, I need cleansing from unrighteousness and doubt of my faith."

"Yes."

"Father, through you, I ask the Holy Spirit to give me enlightenment and a better life. I want the power to resist temptation. I have considered stealing my husband's money from the bank. I know stealing is a sin in the eyes of God. He has millions of dollars in my bank account. He uses me to hide his money from investigators."

"How else have you sinned, my child?"

"Father, I know I have not been a good wife. It has been over three years since I cuddled my husband and comforted him. There is no love and tenderness. What am I supposed to do?"

"Has your husband been faithful to you?"

"No, Father."

"Does he treat you the way a husband should treat a wife?"

"No, Father."

"Well my child, do not accept responsibility. Your husband should share the obligation for this. You need forgiveness for your own actions. The actions you can control. You cannot receive forgiveness for the acts of your husband."

"Thank you, Father. For that I ask the Lord for forgiveness."

"Try not to put too much strain on yourself, my child."

"Thank you for your wisdom, Father."

"Do you promise to follow the Lord?"

"I promise."

"Resist temptation and have faith in the Lord to carry you through these trying times. The Lord will show you a way. You will do your God-given duties again soon. Do not despair."

"Thank you, Father."

"I absolve you of your sins in the Father's name, and of the Son and the Holy Spirit."

They make the sign of the cross.

"Go in peace to love and serve the Lord."

"Thanks be to God."

Michelle genuflects before exiting the confessional.

***

Jules shakes himself awake in the chair at the hospital intensive care unit. He looks at his mother lying on the bed attached to a monitor, a ventilator, and a mobile drip stand.

"Not a word in eighteen days," he mutters to himself.

He comes every morning before work, hoping she says something. Maybe she'll stand and ask to go home, but she lies there resolutely. A pale waxlike look has replaced her once embracing smile.

A nurse walks into the room. Jules stands.

"You can stay, Mr. Bourne. I am checking her vitals," she says.

He sits.

"What are her chances?" he asks.

"It's hard to tell. I have seen people wake after twenty days, sometimes months."

"Hope and pray," he says.

"Add tender care," she says, picking up the chart at the foot of the bed.

"Do you like nursing?" he asks.

"Can't do anything else," she replies.

"I am an engineer," he says.

"I know. I have always wondered why you didn't focus more attention on upgrading the facilities at this hospital. You are responsible for the development and maintenance of the infrastructure of this country," she says accusingly.

"It's not that simple," he says.

"How you mean? You guys find the money to do everything else except fix this hospital. It's two years since the elevator stopped working," she claims.

"You climb those stairs every day?" he asks.

"I must. Do you know how we got your mother up here?" She pauses from entering notes into the chart and looks at him.

"I wondered."

"The orderlies carried her. Fortunately, she has lost weight. When we have a heavy patient, we leave the person downstairs. We cannot get them to the ICU," she says.

"Do you guys report these things to the administration?" he asks.

"You've never heard this?" she counters.

"I have seen no reports on this," he claims.

"Well, you are witnessing it now. I am here every day except my days off. You will leave when your mother leaves. My staff remain to help patients suffering from a range of complications: patients struggling to breathe on makeshift ventilators, people lying here with teary and fearful eyes and no visitors, young and old," she says.

"I am sorry," he says softly, tears welling up in his eyes.

"I am not trying to make you feel bad," she says.

"I understand," he says.

"I must tell you about our working conditions. We believe that people like you don't care. That's how you come across. You show no sympathy for our daily experiences. We work one foot away from the patients. We share their pain and struggle when they're shivering from high fevers and sleepless nights. Minister, you need people who care for others. Workers need facilities to perform," she says.

"I am sorry," Jules apologizes.

"Then do something. We need protective gear, gowns, suits, masks, gloves. Workers carry disinfectant, sanitizers, and cleaning solutions from home. This is really the first time you are hearing this?" she asks.

"Yes," he says.

"Do something," she demands.

His mother groans and babbles unintelligible sounds.

"Does that mean she is hearing us?" he asks.

"She is hearing us. She can't answer," the nurse says.

"Can you wake her up?" he asks.

"It is better like this. They sedated her. People can get excited and anxious if they wake," she says.

"She is trying to say something," Jules says.

"Let us see," the nurse says. She reaches for a small notepad and a pen. She places it into Jules's mother's hand.

Jules watches as his mother uses her left hand to scrawl on the paper. After fifteen minutes she stops, and the pen and pad fall to the ground. He retrieves them and tears off the sheet his mother wrote on. He deciphers the scrawl.

"Raped. Karl is your brother."

CHAPTER ELEVEN

A dark-colored sedan sneaks along the road leading to Nelson Marina. Jules looks out of the car to see an assortment of motorboats and yachts anchored in the tranquil water. The car comes to a halt at one of the parking bays. Jules steps out of the rear seat and strides toward one of the jetties.

His driver follows him to a power launch. He removes his shoes, and one of the crew helps him board the yacht.

He hands his shoes to the driver, who walks back to the car park.

Jules steps into the cabin of the luxury launch engulfed in darkness.

"Welcome on board, minister," the captain greets him.

"Thank you," Jules replies.

"Please make yourself comfortable," the captain requests.

Jules looks around and goes for a seat toward the middle of the power launch. He settles down and straps himself in. The engine purrs into motion, and the boat eases off the jetty.

The captain senses Jules's discomfort.

"My assistant is at the wheel. He is capable," he tells Jules. "Will you have a drink?"

"I would love to, but I can't. I get sick on boats."

"Try to relax. Tension and fear cause the stomach to get upset when riding on the sea. Give me the coordinates for the rendezvous."

Jules fiddles around in his pocket, pulls out a piece of paper, and hands it to the captain, who pulls a small light from his pocket and reads the paper.

"Excuse me a moment. I will be back."

"Fine."

The captain goes up to the wheelhouse and hands his assistant the paper. He returns to keep Jules company.

"Shouldn't be long. We are going to the edge of Mabuya's territorial waters. Forty-five minutes. The water gets choppy but nothing drastic."

"I took seasickness medication and didn't eat."

"I am going to check on my assistant. If you need me, use the radio."

The captain leaves Jules strapped in and staring into the night as the launch rumbles toward the rendezvous point.

***

The bedside clock shows 2:00 a.m. Karl is tossing and turning, while Michelle is asleep next to him. He dreams he is walking through the city of Mabuya surrounded by two security officers.

He greets people in the main vendors' market along the way.

"Boss, how things going?" one vendor asks.

"You tell me."

"Well, look at us. We here struggling in the hot sun. When you go finish this place?"

"We're working hard on it, sister."

"Boss, over four years now since they trying to fix this place."

"Hold strain, sister."

"Boss, doh worry with dem; the election is yours."

"Yes, sister. Thank you."

He browses the market, trying to greet everyone.

The peace and calm of the early morning shatters. People scatter and flee the market opening a path in front of Karl. He begins fighting and shouting in his sleep beside Michelle, who doesn't budge.

Ras appears in the open space armed with a short butcher's machete. Before the security men can react, Ras floats in the air toward Karl with the machete thrust forward in front of him.

As the airborne figure approaches Karl, he flicks his wrist, swiping the machete across Karl's throat, severing his carotid artery and spraying blood all over the place. Ras disappears into the terrain just as he'd come.

The security men rush toward Karl as he falls to the ground. Karl is dead before they catch him and lower him to the concrete surface in the market.

Karl sits up in bed, shaking. Fear grips him. His breathing is rapid and uncontrolled. Sweat fogs his eyes. Distressed and impaired, he throws off the cover and dashes to the bathroom, bumping into walls on his way there.

In the bathroom mirror, he closes his eyes at his ghostly reflection and splashes his face with cold water. Karl walks to the kitchen and makes a hot drink and carries it to his home office. He sits and dials a number.

"I am offering you the post of foreign minister," he says.

"Why would I accept that?" Victor asks, barely awake.

"That is the best I can offer you."

"You're not in a position to offer anything. You are losing this election. I will be the next prime minister."

"At least I made you an offer."

"Karl, you are delusional. Go back to bed and hug your wife."

"My day has started. I will not go back to bed."

"You are obsessed with power."

"I am focused."

"You are only fooling yourself. The people know you suffer from depression and insomnia. They have seen your terrible mood swings, and they detest it. You are like Dr. Jekyll and Mr. Hyde. You make love like a cock or a ram goat, without pleasure. Political power for you is your ability to suppress and manipulate others. This call is to remind me of your power. You know I will not join you. You want to remind me that you're in charge. Waking me up from my sleep because you cannot sleep. Examine yourself, man. Despite all your money and power, you are unhappy. Your emissary failed to recruit me; now you think you can do it yourself. Get a life, man." Victor slams the phone into its cradle.

***

The assistant crewman cuts speed and cruises the boat through the dark and unforgiving ocean. The captain returns to the cabin to check on his passenger.

"We are close," he tells Jules, who is pale and sick.

"Great."

"Stretch your legs."

Jules unstraps himself and follows the captain outside the cabin. The cool breeze and the light ocean spray refresh him. He relaxes in the mysterious stillness of the ocean in the dead of the night. The assistant signals to the captain.

"We are there."

A bright light strikes them, and a luxury yacht pulls up alongside them. The yacht's rear light illuminates the steps, The assistant tosses a rope to the sailor on board the yacht, who secures it to rear.

Jules is holding on to the railing when a hand reaches out and plucks him onto the steps.

Jules enters the yacht from the rear. A sailor pulls him toward the flight of four steps leading to an entrance. The interior of the yacht is well lit despite its darkened exterior. He walks into the living room of a modern floating home. A hundred-inch flat-screen television is showing the news on one wall to the left, and above the bar anther sixty-inch screen is on American football.

"Welcome home." Milosevic stands to greet him.

"This is really a home," Jules states.

"Let's have a drink by the bar," Milosevic says.

"I will have a cup of tea," Jules says.

"Barman, I will have a Drambuie, and draw a tea for my minister," Milosevic says. "How do you take your tea?"

"Black. No sugar, no cream."

"She can accommodate up to fourteen guests. There are five double cabins and two master bedrooms. All cabins come with entertainment center and washroom facilities. Gourmet meals are provided by our on-board chef, with the restaurant being open twenty-four hours. During the day we go on deck for sunbathing and relaxation. I am sorry you couldn't spend more time with us."

"I am tempted."

"Good. Let me entice you more. Each bedroom allows you to see the sea while lying on your bed. Our lighting system can be regulated by your mood and desires. You would notice that the craft is dark from the outside although well lit on the inside. We have the latest in technology catering to iPads, stereo systems, Bluetooth, and wireless headphones."

The men sip their drinks.

"I like fine dining," Jules says.

"Our chef is first class. He takes individual requests and changes his menus by the hour. Give him the material and he works with it. The staff loves to decorate the tables with the finest in porcelain and glassware. Follow me."

Jules follows Milosevic down a set of stairs into a chill room. He sees a wide assortment of wines.

"We stock from every country," Milosevic says. "Ask for it and we give it to you."

The men walk farther on into a tunnel emerging in an aquarium room. A wide species of fish swim in the glass tanks.

"Wow. I have always wanted an aquarium in my home. But this, this is incredible," Jules stutters.

"These fish are not for show," Milosevic says. "We eat them straight from the water. On a barbecue night this the best fish for preparation."

"This is my life when I retire." Jules is gleeful.

"Do not wait until you retire. Live in the moment. After you win the election, I will be back on the island to finish my project. This boat will be available to you and Karl to have all the fun you want—sailing in the open waters, sportfishing, scuba diving. Have you ever done underwater Jet Skiing? Whatever you guys decide to do is fine with me. Take time off from running the government."

"Before I get carried away and remain here, please give me what I came for." Jules shakes himself from his dream.

"Of course."

Jules follows Milosevic to the living room. One of the sailors enter with a huge military bag and drops it on the floor.

Milosevic addresses Jules: "Tell him it's all there. There will be more after he comes to power."

They shake hands. The sailor follows Jules, carrying the bag up the stairs and toward the rear of the yacht.

Jules returns to the small craft. The sailor tosses the bag on board and unties the rope holding the boats together.

"That's it?" the captain asks.

"That's it."

He signals to the assistant, who turns the launch around and increases power for the journey home.

Jules cradles the bag as he reenters the cabin to resume his seat.

***

Rita and Karl are sitting across the table from Dr. Blunt once more.

"I have your results, prime minister," Dr. Blunt pauses.

"Well?" Karl asks.

"You sure you don't want your wife to be here?" Dr. Blunt asks.

Rita glares at the doctor.

The doctor clears his throat.

"My mother is here, Dr. Blunt.

Dr. Blunt passes a photo to Karl.

"This is from the scan. If you look at the corner toward the bottom of the stem of the brain, you will see it. It's small but growing. Can you see it?" The doctor points to the scan.

"Yes," Karl says.

"It is too small to operate on," Dr. Blunt explains.

What do you suggest?"

"We leave it alone and watch it."

"And the sleeping problem?" Karl asks.

"That is easy. I will give you something that helps you sleep," the doctor says.

"You mean to have me drowsy all the time?" Karl pouts.

"No. The medication will give you a full night's sleep. The next day you will be normal," the doctor claims.

"What dangers does this pose?" Karl asks.

"This is new to me. I suggest that you see a brain specialist as soon as you travel. The symptoms can affect your motor skills and muscle tone. It can lead to a deterioration in the motor neurons and result in a form of Lou Gehrig's disease."

"Lou Gehrig?"

"It paralyzes you."

"I told you they were dipping they hand in your blood," Rita shouts. "They want to cripple you."

Dr. Blunt looks at Rita in contempt.

"Doc, thanks for your help once again." Karl shakes his hand. "I will see a specialist soon."

"I agree," the doctor says.

"You have been great, doc. Real great."

Rita and Karl leave the room.

*****

At the Catholic cathedral, Karl is kneeling in front of a small altar decorated for a special ceremony. Kenny kneels on Karl's right, holding his hand. On his left, Rita has a firm grip on him while massaging her rosary.

The bishop approaches from an inner chamber dressed in his full ceremonial robe and swinging an incense thurible from side to side. As the bishop approaches, the trio, swathed in frankincense smoke, mumble incoherently to themselves.

The bishop places the thurible at the back of the altar and picks up a vial of holy water. He walks around them sprinkling the holy water and praying softly.

Kenny and Rita tighten their grip on Karl as they feel him sliding away. Rita turns to Karl, her eyes watery.

"I love you, my son," she says.

Kenny echoes: "I love you, brother. I am with you."

Karl gets up to run away. They clutch him and he falls to the ground, convulsing. He eases his back against the altar and becomes still, his eyes glazed and staring blankly.

The bishop walks toward him as Kenny and Rita hold him.

"You shall repeat after me. In the name of Jesus..."

"In the name of Jesus..." Karl repeats.

"I, Karl Stone..."

"I, Karl Stone..."

"...ask to silence and expel evil."

"...ask to silence and expel evil."

"I command that they leave now."

"I command that they leave now."

An awful roar fills the room, and loud footsteps hurry toward the exit. The door opens and slams shut, then the noise subsides.

The bishop backs away from Karl and heads for the altar. He clutches his rosary and places one hand on the Bible.

"I ask you, Jesus, to cast evil spirits from our brother Karl." He clasps his hands in prayer. "Thank you, Lord. In Jesus's name, I command that the evil spirits shall not return. Blessed be to Karl in the name of the Father, the Son, and the Holy Spirit."

The bishop moves in closer to Karl and rests his hands on his head.

"There is evil around you. Close to you. You need to expel it. This part only you can do. Look around you; the Holy Spirit will show you the way."

The bishop steps back to look at Karl.

"Peace be with you, my son."

He backs away from Karl and into the inner chamber from where he had entered.

***

Karl and Kenny are at the bar in Karl's living room. Karl is drinking scotch while Kenny is sipping red wine.

"The ground ain't looking so good," Kenny says.

"The polling showing ugly," Karl responds.

"How many seats?"

"Two. Mine and another one."

Kenny gets off his stool, sips the wine, and leans against the bar.

"Wow," Kenny says. "What happened?"

"Lazy candidates have not done their work."

"I thought you made drastic changes."

"Yes, but the replacements are worse."

There is a knock on the door. Swaggart pokes his head through.

"Minister Jules is here, boss."

"Tell him to come."

Jules enters the room carrying the heavy bag from the boat.

"I didn't open it."

"Fine, just rest it in the corner over there."

Jules hauls the bag to the place Karl indicates and drops it, relieved.

"Everything went well."

"Did anyone follow you?"

"Never."

"Kenny and I are taking a drink. Do you want one?"

"Nah. I must go. I must go home."

"Okay, then."

Jules stops before he walks out the door.

"The ground looks rough."

"Why do you say that?"

"Everything shows we are losing."

"You must not repeat that crap."

"I am just telling you what I picked up on the ground; my analysis is the same."

"Jules, I know you are tired. Go home and rest yourself, and stop peddling that bullshit."

"You're the boss."

Before Jules could close the door, Karl catches up with him and taps him on the shoulder.

"On your way out, fire Swaggart."

"Fire him?"

"Yes. Fire him."

"Okay."

In the yard, Jules signals to two of the security officers and pulls them off to one side for a short conversation. The two men walk to Swaggart and speak to him.

Swaggart pushes the men away and walks briskly toward the house. Jules bars him from going in.

"That is not a good idea," Jules says.

"What did I do?" Swaggart protests. "He has to tell me why."

"No, he doesn't. He is the prime minister for God's sake."

The other officers escort Swaggart out of the yard.

Jules gets into his car and speeds away.

In the living room, Karl returns to the bar to find Kenny baffled and shaken. He pours another stiff scotch and refills Kenny's wine.

"What was that?"

"Don't look so worried."

"I am not. However…"

"Never listen to this shit. They will peddle it further and claim they discussed it with you. You need to stop them in their tracks early."

"And Swaggart?"

"He is acting strangely. He is dissatisfied and unhappy."

"The bag?"

"I cannot spend this amount on the election knowing I am losing. I hope you take care of the remainder."

Kenny relaxes and smiles. There are things he would do for his brother without question.

"That's my job."

***

Yellow serves a customer a plate of food, then goes to the back of the shop for another. He emerges with the second plate of manicou, steamed bananas, yam, and dumplings.

"Dunno how you do it," one man says.

"Do what?" Yellow asks.

"Ah want to lick the plate," the man claims.

"If you want seconds, there is more." Yellow laughs.

"Let me take a drink," the man says.

Yellow continues to dish out food to the men in the shop.

"Yellow, what is your secret recipe?" another man asks.

"If I tell you, I will have to shoot you." Yellow grins.

"I eat manicou and steamed food in different places, but nothing compares to yours," the man continues.

"Yellow, don't tell them. They go use it against you," a woman says.

"Darling, even though I tell them, they can't do it," Yellow brags.

"Let hear it!" the men shout.

"It starts with the wood. You want a hardwood. It must not be too green or too dry. The wood must give off smoke. Smoke is a part of the flavor of the food. The woodsmoke must not overpower the food's taste. You need wood that turns into coals as the food cooks. This slows the fire and allows your food to cook from the inside out," Yellow explains.

He serves a customer.

"That's it?" the customers tease.

"All right. You've been loyal customers; you deserve a peek into my secrets. Seasoning is the other crucial factor. I start with sea salt. None of that manufactured crap. Before you apply the salt, you must wash your meat thoroughly. Drain out the blood. Cooking with blood is dangerous. It is a way of transferring diseases and viruses. Vinegar and flour will do the trick. Then you rub in the sea salt. At that point she is ready to accept your seasoning. I make my own local stuff—a blend of chives, thyme, mint, lemongrass, ginger, paprika, basil, and shadow benny. Pour the mixture onto the meat, and rub it in. Things like seasoning pepper, onion, and garlic, you add to the pot while it's cooking."

He serves another customer.

"Yellow, you holding back on us," a customer says.

"All what I give you already? Come on, man. Okay, pay attention to your fire. Brown your meat to an even color, and pour in boiling water from a separate pot. Bring to boil rapidly, then lower your fire, allowing the meat to cook. Place the correct amount of water to steam the food. Remember, they call it steam food and not boil food. Allow the water to warm, then throw in your dumplings. Pack your yam and bananas on top, and cover," Yellow explains.

"I thought you put the dumplings on top?" a customer says.

"Popular mistake. Dumplings cannot overcook, but they can under-cook. Yam and bananas mash up at the bottom of the pot, while the dumplings are still cooking."

"Now we know how you do it," a woman says.

"Don't copy me. I told you the ingredients, but you don't have my special touch," Yellow boasts.

"I will try your way," the woman says.

"Make sure you have some bread and ham and cheese to make sand-wiches in case you screw up the food." Yellow chuckles.

"Yellow, you know she can't cook," another man says.

"Everybody knows." Yellow laughs.

"So, what you think about the final stretch?" a customer asks.

"Let me read it to you," Yellow says. He opens the newspaper and reads aloud.

In our final article before the election, we warn the ruling Mabuya National Party (MNP) not to believe that a victory is a fait accompli. Ruling parties before went into an election confident of victory only to end up with egg on their faces on the big day.

The MNP itself came to power fifteen years ago when the then MDM administration thought it was home with a certain election victory. They called an election against the background of economic strength and recovery from a structural adjustment program that had worked for them. The finance minister and leader of the party at the time, a self-styled economic guru, convinced the party members and followers that the medicine he'd dished out during the previous five years had worked and the nation was poised for takeoff. He had a rude awakening on the day of the election, losing to the opposition by one parliamentary seat. He retired from politics.

The MDM had campaigned on the back of its economic gains and the ability and strength of the finance minister to consolidate these gains. They said the election results were a foregone conclusion. They are still recovering from the shock of that night.

The MNP continued MDM's economic program guided by the International Monetary Fund (IMF). They made bold moves, including the removal of income tax, making the economic indicators stronger. They recorded low inflation, low unemployment, a stable exchange rate, and rising international reserves.

However, on the eve of this election, MNP is in the position MDM found itself in fifteen years ago. The party is arrogant and aloof, is a victim of its own lies. They believe they cannot lose the election.

The MNP is underestimating the effect of a new specter haunting the minds of the voters in this election—dishonesty in public office. This was not present in the last election. Talk abounds of members of the ruling party collecting millions of dollars from characters of dubious standing in society. When this newspaper confronted the prime minster about the Milosevic case, he said he wished there were more Milosevics in the world.

The voters understand the economic "good news," but they don't understand or agree with the "how." The party die-hards are in full stride. This, however, is not sufficient to win an election. The party needs 20 percent of the swing and undecided votes to push it over the line. The last poll shows the two parties in a dead heat with 30 percent of registered voters either undecided or not voting. This is not good for the MNP.

It is worse for Karl Stone as he approaches the twilight of his political career. It is doubtful that he can withstand the rigors of five years in opposition to return to the polls as an octogenarian. The last two octogenarians in regional politics were Juan Bosh and Joaquin Balaguer in the Dominican Republic during the 1980s.

It is also known that the way Karl has ruled the MNP, micromanaging a one-man decision-making center and refusing to groom generational succession, will mean its demise as a political force in Mabuya.

The closest man to the leader of the party is Jules Bourne, who may at best have five years of leadership given his age and could face money-laundering and other charges along with Karl for accepting and handling huge sums of cash from known and unknown sources. This newspaper has obtained a witness statement given by an onlooker whose identity is being withheld for security reasons. We produce a shortened version of this statement below:

"I took Minister Bourne to the ocean in my boat. We traveled into the night for ten minutes where we met a larger vessel. We collected a heavy canvas bag, then the larger vessel disappeared into the night.

"The Minister sat for a while, then opened the canvas bag and extracted a wad of cash, which he placed into his jacket pocket. He dug into the bag a second time, extracting a smaller wad of cash, which he gave to me. I dropped the minister to shore, where he took the bag and entered a motor vehicle."

This is a chilling indictment on the minister. We believe this matter will escalate when the ruling party loses power.

In our opinion, with the current trend, the demise of the ruling party will make way for the development of a third force in the politics of this country. Younger people will have to step up and take charge of their destiny. They cannot depend on the elders to pave a way for them. The gains of the recent structural adjustment program are already disappearing as world economic conditions change. Past efforts at containing the economy and placing the island on a sustainable economic footing have been wiped out.

The prime minister must accept full responsibility for the upcoming defeat. This newspaper has rebuked Karl for his blunders—adultery, dishonesty, lies, and disarray. We expose him as a failure. Karl has been steadfast in maintaining his course. He refuses to seek and accept advice. The opposition has offered to help and collaborate in the implementation of stalled programs. He has refused. We agree with the opposition's call for change and the engagement of the community and stakeholders to discuss and plan the future of this country.

Karl has ruled the party and government with an iron fist. His dictatorial ways have ostracized ministers and other people closest to him, even his wife.

Probably after fifty years in politics, this is a good time for him to go home and make peace with his wife.

Yellow lowers the newspaper as a deafening silence envelops the bar.

***

Karl arrives in the yard, leaves the car, and climbs the few stairs into the polling station. His security team deploys to stand guard.

The procedure inside is quick and silent. An election official identifies him. She checks his name on the voters' list, hands him the ballot paper, and ushers him into the private voting booth.

Karl returns from the booth with his folded ballot, shows it to the supervisor, and places it into the ballot box. He dips his index finger in the ink well and exits the building.

As he crosses the yard, several journalists await him.

"Prime minister, have you voted?"

"Yes, I have."

"How do you view your chances?"

"My party has a good chance of winning."

"What are your plans if you lose?"

Karl pauses to survey the gathering.

"You know it's illegal to campaign today," he snaps at the journalist.

Karl gets in the car, and his driver pulls out of the yard.

***

Richard is sitting on a flowered towel with his back propped against the open trunk of his vehicle. Diana is lying with her head in his lap, sunglasses hiding her eyes.

His gaze travels over the dark green mountainside down to the white sandy beach and crystal blue waters. They've repacked the picnic basket, and a half bottle of red wine sits in a cooling tub next to the basket.

"Did you grow up doing this?" he asks, pointing to the sea and the landscape.

"No. As a child I didn't have the luxury of exposure to the finer aspects of life," she says.

"Then why do you love it so?" he asks.

"Deprival," she answers.

"That is true. People tend to enjoy the relaxation and enjoyment they were denied in their youth. Given the ability to enjoy them now, they take full advantage," he says.

"My parents had love. They still do. But no money," she claims.

"Love was enough," Richard says.

"Not for me. I want more. I want everything. Here and now." Diana is firm.

"Deprivation," Richard mutters.

Diana becomes quiet and Richard plays with her short hair. He reflects on his assumptions about her when she was assigned to him during his first job on Mabuya Island. Diana turned out to be an extrovert—ambitious and competitive. She was imaginative, charming, and reckless.

They worked together well. Her assertive approach to problem-solving was valuable in completing their assignments. Where she lacked experience and knowledge, she compensated with energy and drive.

The agency paid well, and this allowed her to live an above-average lifestyle. She paid for her active and vivacious daily living without caring for the approval of others.

Richard realized that Diana's materialistic way of life distracted attention from her substantive work. Still, it provided her with entry to places he scorned. She had a membership to the golf club, the sailing association, the motor racing club, and the lodge. Yet his opportunism forced him to use her access to gather intelligence on those areas. To become attached to her. A certain amount of indispensability. *Teamwork* he called it.

"I spoke to the agency," he tells her.

"And?"

"They've agreed to release you."

"That was easy," Diana says softly.

"They wanted to reassign you. I had to use my powers."

She sits up, removes her shades, and looks into Richard's eyes. He matches her stare.

"I am retiring too."

"Free at last. You deserve it, Richard."

"What are your plans?"

"You, Diana. You."

Richard pulls a ring box out of his pocket and opens it to show a single-studded diamond ring.

"Will you marry me?" he proposes.

"I will." She smiles.

He kisses her and they roll in the grass.

***

At the MNP party headquarters, several people are milling around; others are working on their laptops and cell phones. One man is sitting at a desktop computer inputting data.

Karl walks over to the computer operator and leans his head over the man.

"Any improvement?"

"The opposition has six out of six so far."

"We still have the strongholds to come?"

"I haven't lost hope."

Karl taps him on the shoulder. "Good boy. Keep working at it. Keep working."

He leaves the room and walks out to the verandah, where Jules is sipping a bottle of water while staring at the city lights and the ocean beyond.

"It is not looking good."

"Nope."

"We won't get the numbers."

"Unlikely."

"I am going home."

The men embrace, tapping each other on the back.

"Be careful on the road, man."

"I'll be safe."

"We must meet for an assessment."

"Certainly."

Karl returns to the meeting room. The operator turns around from the computer.

"Boss, I was looking for you."

Karl walks over to the operator.

"Boss, we pull back two."

"Which two?"

"Yours and another one."

Karl frowns and turns away from the operator.

"People, if you need me, call me at home."

Karl leaves the room.

***

The official car followed by a back-up vehicle pull into the yard and stop short of the garage. Karl steps out and walks toward the house. He stops at the front door, facing the security men.

"Guys, thank you for being here for me. You performed beyond the call of duty. Even when you were off duty, you came to help. Thank you."

"Thanks, boss. Rest. Take a vacation."

"Good idea. Take care, guys."

Karl turns and enters the house. He paces, mumbling to himself. His reddened eyes scan the living room. He holds his head in his hands as he retraces the events leading up this point.

A knock on the door interrupts his train of thought. He doesn't move. One of the security men opens it and pokes his head through the opening.

"The colonel wants to see you."

"Let him come."

The man steps aside for Colonel Bynoe to enter the room.

"How you're coping, boss?"

"Getting used to being out of office. Have they made the official announcement?"

"Yes."

"What were the final numbers?"

"They got thirteen; you held on to two."

"Shameful."

"That's why I came here. Don't look at things this way. The party fought hard. You had fifteen years of power. The population wants to try something new."

"To hell with that, Colonel. My people didn't work. I had too many traitors around me."

"Boss, I suggest that you try to rest. Let's do the postmortem next week. Don't be hard on yourself."

"I hear you, Colonel."

Karl hugs Colonel Bynoe before they part. Colonel Bynoe strides past two journalists snooping around the house.

"What are your comments on the election, Colonel Bynoe?" they ask.

"As you know, gentlemen, we lost the election by a sizable margin, and in the coming days, we do the analysis of what occurred."

"How are you feeling now? Cheated?"

"No. Remember, it was a contest, and only one party can win. The next party will obviously lose. No need to be ashamed."

"How is your leader?"

"I spoke to him. He feels the same as I do. As you know, he is a man who throws his energy into his work. I have advised him to get some rest."

"Will he resign from the party?"

"That is not a discussion for now. I have answered your questions; can you let me go now? I am tired too."

Colonel Bynoe bursts his way through the journalists and walks to his vehicle.

***

Karl prepares for bed. He goes to the bathroom, uses the toilet, showers, wraps himself in a huge towel, and drags himself to the bedroom.

In the bedroom, he changes into pajamas. He glares at Michelle, who has turned on her bedside light and is sitting up reading the Bible. He crawls into bed, turns his back to her, and stares at the wall.

"Boss, you need to come here," a guard shouts from the driveway.

Karl sits up in the bed, dazed.

"Boss, you have to come," the man repeats.

"I am not coming," Karl yells.

Michelle pulls on a robe over her nightgown, slips on a pair of bedroom slippers, and walks toward the voice.

At the house entrance, she opens the door to face a uniformed security officer.

"I told them not to disturb the boss. But they insisted."

"That's okay."

The security man steps aside, and behind him is a tall, burly police inspector from the Rapid Response Unit (RRU) dressed in army fatigues, his insignia visible on the lapels of his jacket.

"We have orders to take control of the government assets in your possession."

"We have nothing here. On the contrary, the state has personal items of ours that we will need to collect. I will do so tomorrow."

"I am taking possession of the state vehicles and any other items you have belonging to the state."

"But my husband is still in office. The new prime minister has not been sworn in."

"Ma'am, I am under orders here."

"This is an outrage. You guys are just trying to embarrass my husband. Take all that you want, and get out of here."

"You also need to vacate the premises."

"We will leave tomorrow."

"Miss…"

"The security men have the keys. I am tired and worn out. I am going back to bed."

Michelle turns and walks away.

"Ma'am…"

Michelle glares at the inspector one more time.

"Tomorrow," he confirms.

She returns to the bedroom, kicks off her slippers, and slides in beneath the covers.

She flicks on her night-light and gets back to her Bible. She opens the marked page—Leviticus 26:17—and mumbles the verse.

"I will turn against you so that you will be defeated by your enemies. Those who hate you will rule over you, and you will flee even though no one is pursuing you."

Karl is unable to sleep. He stares at the walls for a while as his eyes fill with tears.

"It's all gone," he mutters.

Michelle lowers the Bible and places it on the nightstand.

He turns to face her.

"It's all gone. Everything is gone. Everybody is gone." He sobs.

Michelle opens her arms, and he collapses into them, sobbing beyond control.

"Not all is gone. I am still here. I am still your wife."

She rocks him like a kitten, her mind fixed on the future.

THE END